Crashing Waves

By

Graysen Morgen

2014

Crashing Waves © 2014 Graysen Morgen
Triplicity Publishing, LLC

ISBN-13: 978-0988619678
ISBN-10: 0988619679

This is a work of fiction. Names, characters, places, and incidents are the product of the author's imagination and are used fictitiously. Any resemblance to actual persons, living or dead, business establishments, events of any kind, or locales is entirely coincidental.

Printed in the United States of America
First Edition – 2014

Cover Design: Triplicity Publishing, LLC
Interior Design: Triplicity Publishing, LLC

Also by Graysen Morgen

Acknowledgements

Special thanks to CJ, my eagle eyes down under! *Tack för allt du gör, kompis.*

Dedication

This book is dedicated to my partner. Years ago you asked me to write a surfing book. I'm sorry it has taken me this long to finish it. *Is breá liom tú*

Prologue

December (Pipeline Invitational)

The announcer looked on with fear in his eyes as he watched two pieces of the broken yellow and white surfboard wash ashore. The entire crowd on Oahu's North Shore was standing in silence, watching the massive Bonzai Pipeline waves. The three-time Women's Short Board Surfing World Champion and present leader of the Women's World Championship Tour, Rory Eden, had just wiped out in a shallow zone with razor sharp reefs. She was being held under by the fierce current in what was known as a triple hold-down to surfers around the world, and amounted to nearly two minutes underwater. Two riders on Jet ski's were out in the double-overhead, thirteen foot waves, searching furiously for any sign of the surfer.

"Ladies and gentlemen, it appears that Rory Eden is still being pulled under by the brutal Pipeline waves. No surfer has ever survived a triple hold-down in this area.

She is a very strong young woman and it's possible that she..."

Just as he paused, trying to gather his words, the rescue crew found the surfer being torn between the waves. They quickly hauled her limp body to shore. Two paramedics put Rory on a backboard and shuffled her into the back of the ambulance, before anyone standing on the beach could see her. Once inside the rescue vehicle, the paramedics performed CPR until they were able to finally get her heart beating, but her pulse was very weak and fading in and out. One of the medics squeezed the oxygen bag that was manually breathing for her while the other went to work trying to stop the bleeding from the massive cut across the top left side of her head.

"Her body is in severe shock. She has a four inch laceration on the left side of her crania and we had to do chest compressions three times from the beach front to here. I don't know how much longer she can hold on," the paramedic said, squeezing the bag and filling her lungs with air as he handed her over to the flight nurse.

The helicopter transported her to The Queens Medical Center in Honolulu. Rory's cold, limp body was immediately taken into the trauma center from the helicopter pad.

"Let's intubate and get her stabilized, then send her up to get a CT scan. Also alert the neurosurgeon on call," the male doctor said, squeezing the bag as they raced into the brightly lit room.

"Doctor, she's arresting!" the nurse said, watching the heart monitor bounce all over the screen.

"Damn it, start CPR." He grabbed the defibrillator. "Two hundred, CLEAR!" he yelled.

Everyone watched as the heartbeat on the monitor was still jumping around erratically.

"Two fifty, CLEAR! Come on, girl!"

"No change!" the nurse yelled.

"Two seventy, CLEAR!"

"The pulse is weak, but her rhythm's normal."

"We need to intubate and stabilizer her now! God damn it. Where in the hell is the neurosurgeon? This girl needs her head closed. She's starting to bleed out!" He replaced the blood-soaked bandage on her head.

"Start a line of saline and B positive. We have to get this bleeding under control!"

"Doctor, the neurosurgeon's on line one."

"Get your ass down here! I have a critical head trauma on my table with a four inch laceration that is bleeding out on the left side! Either you come down and sew her head or I'm doing it my goddamn self. This girl's going to die if we don't get her stabilized!" he yelled into the phone.

~ ~ ~

Two Weeks Later

"Hi, Mrs. Eden. I'm Rory's doctor," the neurosurgeon said. He was tall and lanky and his scrub top looked a little too big.

"Is she getting any better?" An attractive, slender blond woman replied with a heavy Australian accent.

"She's showing some signs of muscular activity and her neurological waves are functioning very close to normal. We're still not sure if there is any significant brain damage from the loss of blood and lack of oxygen," he answered.

"When will I be able to take her back to California?"

"As her physician, I cannot advise that she be moved at this time. She's still in a comatose state and not breathing completely on her own. When and if she wakes up, Rory is going to need around the clock care and eventually a large amount physical therapy."

"What exactly are you saying doctor?" *I'm not stupid, you dickhead!*

"Well, Mrs. Eden, you know I have been honest with you from the beginning."

"I shouldn't have to inform you again that my last name is Zane, not Eden."

"Yes, my apologies, Ms Zane. Her body is in shock. Rory's brain shut down from the trauma of the injury and lack of oxygen. In turn, the rest of her organs slowly followed until nothing was functioning. This is often the case with severe head trauma or drowning. A number of patients regain control of their bodies and fully recover. Like I have said before, she could come out of this coma and be just as normal as she was before the accident, but then there is a possibility that your daughter may never wake up at all," he paused.

"When she does wake up, she could be in a vegetative state for the rest of her life. Also, there is always a third possibility, Rory could wake up with only minor neurological damage. In that case she may need to learn how to walk, talk, and eat again, but there is a good chance she would recover completely."

~ ~ ~

Six Weeks After The Accident

"Doctor, my daughter has been in a coma for over a month now. Bloody hell! Tell me something other than you're waiting for her to wake up."

"Ms. Zane, you have to be patient with this. We have done everything we can do at this point. It really is up to Rory now. She is a very strong young woman, mentally and physically. Her body was put through a major ordeal. She's very lucky to still be alive."

"I sit here next to this bed and talk to her every day and she has never moved a muscle. She has a tube in her throat breathing for her and a tube in her side feeding her. Tell me, could you sit here and watch your child like this? I don't know how much more of it I can take."

~ ~ ~

Six Weeks & A Day After The Accident

"Doctor! Nurse! Hello, anybody, she's opened her eyes. She's awake!" Rory's mother ran into the hallway screaming.

The doctor raced into the room. "Rory, can you hear me? Squeeze my finger if you can hear me," he said, grabbing her hand.

"Can she hear you, doctor? Please tell me, is she okay?"

"Ms. Zane, I need you to wait out in the hall and I'll come see you in a few minutes. Rory, blink your eyes if you can hear me," the doctor spoke without looking up.

"Damn it, she's not registering what I'm saying. Rory, can you see me? Blink your eyes if you can see me." The doctor shined a pen light near her eyes, checking her pupils.

"Her eyes aren't moving at all," the nurse said.

"She's confused. Her brain doesn't know where she is or what's going on. We need to pull the tube out." He listened to her chest quickly, then pulled the tube from her throat.

Rory coughed and gasped for second as he listened to her lungs again. "Her respirations and heartbeat are normal," he said, making notes in her chart. "Rory, I'm your doctor and I'm here to help you. Don't try to talk. We'll work on that later. I need you to blink your eyes if you can hear me." He waited as she slowly closed her light blue eyes and opened them once again. "Excellent, now blink again if you can see me." He watched her blink once more.

"Good, that's very good. Now, can you squeeze my finger?" He watched her fingers move slightly, unable to close around his. "That's okay, your muscles haven't been working in a while, but you're doing very well. One more thing and I'll leave you alone. Wiggle your toes for me." He stared at her feet. "Alright, it looks like our only form of communication right now is blinking, so let's try once for yes and twice for no. I'm going to step out of the room, but I'll be right back."

"Ms. Zane, everything looks good," he said, walking up to the woman who was leaning against the wall with a blank look on her face. "She's blinking her eyes, so she can see and hear me and she seems to understand what I'm saying. Her body hasn't been moving on its own and she's stiff, so she can't wiggle her toes yet. However, she did move her fingers a little bit. I'll know more in a day or two after we run some tests, but this is a very good sign."

Chapter One

December (four years after the accident)

The alarm clock buzzed loudly at four a.m., sending Rory into a fit. Ripping at the covers on her king-sized bed, she reached out in the dark, fumbling for it on the nightstand to shut off the noise. Laying her head back down, she closed her eyes tightly one last time, before climbing out of the bed, stretching her arms high above her head and yawning at the thought of a new day. *Just once I'd like to sleep in. God, I'm not asking for the whole day, just an hour or two without interruption. No dreams, no deadlines, no worries, no alarm clock!*

Ten minutes later, she was downstairs, dressed in warm-up pants and a sports bra and lacing up her Nike sneakers. She threw on a small wind breaker, before heading through the French doors, across the deck, past the pool, and out onto the sandy beach that she called her backyard. Her white, two-story modern-style beach house, sat oceanfront at the end of a small winding driveway in a high class part of Long Beach, California.

Her property was just over two acres, which was rather small for the area, yet gigantic to her, a woman who lived alone and preferred it. Most of her property was actually the private beach behind her house.

She jogged for a few miles, and then slowed to a walk, peering out into the moonlit waves. It was at that moment that she took off in a sprint, running as hard and as fast as she could before turning around to head back home. She never changed her pace until she was directly behind her house. She came to a jolting stop, and then walked across the deck, around the pool and through the French doors.

The steaming shower slowly erased the morning irritation, along with the sand and salt air from Rory's golden tanned skin and muscular frame. She towel dried her short, ash-blond hair before styling it in a slightly messy, yet still moderately sophisticated look. The long scar on the left side of her head had faded somewhat, but was still visible through her light hair. She'd kept the white terry cloth robe wrapped around her as she walked downstairs to the kitchen, opening the stainless steel door of the refrigerator. Her baby blue eyes glanced around at the lack of food on the shelves. Grabbing the jug of orange juice, she poured the last of its contents into the largest glass she could find. She then smeared a small amount of cream cheese on a plain bagel and sat silently at the breakfast bar on the side of the island in the center of the kitchen. She'd skipped her morning Tai Chi routine hoping an extra couple of miles added to her run would help calm her.

At six o'clock she was dressed casually in khaki pants, a white polo shirt emblazoned with a logo of a surfboard and a snowboard crisscrossing embroidered above her right breast and brown slip-on canvas shoes that looked like a cross between boat shoes and an old man's house shoes. She pulled a light blue hoodie on over her head, with the same logo printed across the front, and grabbed a worn brown leather briefcase from the study on her way out.

~ ~ ~

The sun had yet to show its first signs of rising as the midnight blue Audi R8 Spyder, backed slowly out of the two car garage. Rory shifted gears and turned the sports car, heading down the winding driveway with the convertible top down and an old Melissa Etheridge CD blaring from the speakers. She pushed the console button as she neared the eight foot tall iron gates.

Twenty five miles along the interstate and thirty minutes of traffic later, she arrived in the parking garage of the three-story, steel framed building in Los Angeles that she referred to as her 'home away from home'. Eden Boards, LLC. was what the large block style lettering spelled on all four sides of the building, as well as above the large doors at the main floor entrance. Rory stepped out of her car with her briefcase and cell phone as she pushed the auto-lock button on her key ring and walked through the main entrance of her million dollar corporation, a worldwide surf and snowboard design and manufacturing company.

The security guard, front desk receptionist, and a few of the staff members that worked on the second floor in the research and design department, were the only employees to ever arrive as early as Rory.

As Rory stepped off the elevator on the third floor, her charismatic, short skirt wearing, secretary, Alexandra Walker, stopped her.

"Good morning, Rory. Martie has arrived early today."

Rory spoke with a slight Australian accent. "Is that right? She must have something up her sleeve to beat me into the office. Thanks, Alex."

Rory walked into her ridiculously large office, laying her briefcase down on the large black metal desk next to the flat screen computer monitor. Along the wall to the left, was a massive bookcase that matched her desk with closed cabinets at both ends. The other wall had been covered with framed photos and magazine covers. A floor to ceiling window ran along the wall behind the desk. Rory sat down in her leather chair and turned on her computer monitor. Before she could log in to check her e-mail folder, she heard a half knock at the door. She looked up to see one of the most beautiful, yet extremely eccentric, people she'd ever met, walk in.

Martina Cruz had been Rory's best friend of over ten years, as well as the vice president of the company. She was nearly the same height as Rory, but with long, wavy black hair just passed her shoulders, olive colored skin, and chocolate brown eyes as bright as her smile. She was dressed similarly in attire. The company dress code was casual, but slightly business casual with a surfer flare.

"Martie, I see you've decided to come to work on time this morning. What could have possibly brought you in here before the sun came up? No, wait don't tell me, let me guess? You're having a mid life crisis at twenty seven? Or hmm…."

11

"Rory, come on, don't do this to yourself. It's been four years. I'm here for you. I know that you know what today is. Don't lie to me and damn it, stop lying to yourself. I can see it in your eyes."

"Martie, I've told you a hundred times, I'm over it. I've been over it for a long time. Can we please move on? I have deadlines to make and we have a meeting with some of the designers this morning. There is no time in my schedule to discuss the past or relive an anniversary. I'm alive and well. Let's move on."

"You want it like that, then fine! I'm here to offer support for you and you shut me away as usual. I love you, I always have and I always will. You're my best friend. Damn it, Rory, my life ended that day too. Can't you see that?"

"Martie, that's enough! I'm busy and unless you have company information to discuss with me, this conversation is over!"

Martie walked out of the office shaking her head. She closed the door, pausing for a long minute, before returning to her own office at the end of the hall. *I see it in you, Rory. You have to face it. One day you will surf again, I know you will. You're so God damn stubborn. I thought I had lost you four years ago today. Don't you think it hurts me too? I thought you were going to die. One day, my friend, you will wake up and realize your life is not over and you're not alone. Not at all.*

~ ~ ~

Rory sat back in her chair with her eyes tightly closed. *Just once I'd like to get through this day without the pain and hurt. Damn you, Martie, for starting in on me first thing in the morning. Let it go, I did.* She sat up, pressing the intercom button on the phone.

"Yes, Rory."

"Alex, let me know when the snow team gets here. I need to meet with them in Conference Room A at nine o'clock."

"Yes ma'am, I'll send down a message. Shall I send Martie a message to attend the meeting as well?"

"By all means, Alex, she *is* my vice president. I would expect her to be at all of my meetings. Thanks."

Rory turned off the intercom and sat back, reading her incoming mail. She was halfway through the messages, when she noticed a suspicious email address from a company she had never heard of. All of the incoming email and other computer shared information were always heavily screened for viruses and other security measures on their server. Even so, she still deleted the message without ever opening it. Her entire company was run on her computer. If a virus were to ever get inside it could ruin her. Of course, there was always snail mail which was why she had an incoming and outgoing box on the corner of her desk. Most of the envelopes in that box were to and from large companies or were regarding surf and snowboard expo events and competitions. She'd finally cleared out her inbox and sent out everything that she'd needed to. Just as she was about to preview the documents for a proposal on a new line of products, the intercom buzzed.

"Rory, the snow team is ready for you."

"Thank you, Alex. Please tell them that I'll be right down."

On the way to the elevator, Martie caught up to

Rory, carrying a small manila folder and a cup of coffee.

"That shit will kill you, you know," Rory chided.

"It's only coffee and besides, I'm an adult. If I want to drink shit, I will. Did you get an email from the Billabong Pro director?" Martie replied.

"No, why? Was I supposed to?"

"Well it went on over the weekend and I had received a letter from them last week saying they'd wanted to give you some kind of achievement award."

"What? I never received anything about that. Oh well, I haven't achieved anything award winning since I left the tour. Did we at least have a representative there with our boards? Just because I don't care to be there in the middle of it doesn't mean my company will suffer."

"Yeah we were there. I sent Greg Underwood. He's been working with Cara Mann. You know the girl that's leading the tour right now."

"Yes, I saw that. Did she re-sign her contract?"

"Of course she did."

The elevator stopped and both women walked down the hall to the first door on the left. A large oval shaped table sat in the middle of the room with two empty seats out of thirty chairs that surrounded it. Rory sat at the head of the table with Martie on her immediate right side. The head of the snowboard design team, Stephen Silver, sat to her left. He was a tall, physically trim guy in his early thirties with dark brown hair.

"Well, I'm glad we could all make it on time this morning. I've called this meeting so that everyone can catch up on the upcoming events. This is the second full week of December and we still have a lot to do before January gets here." She paused to put on her titanium, thin-framed glasses, so that she could read the schedule and documents in the folder that Martie had slid over to her.

"The last weekend of January through the first three days of February is the Winter X Games in Aspen, Colorado. Everyone is well aware that I will be attending these events. I'm excited about the direction we are headed with snowboarding and I'm looking forward to personally meeting Ezekiel Jones, the new snowboarder that we signed. You all know him of course, since you've been working for two months on his prototype boards. Also, coming up in February from the tenth through the twenty sixth is the XXIV Winter Olympic Games in Stockholm, Sweden. I will also be attending those games for about nine days. Stephen please update us on exactly how many riders we've signed for the X Games and the Olympics."

"Yes ma'am, we'll be sponsoring three American men at the X Games and then in the Olympics we have those same three riders since we're in binding contracts with them, as well as twenty more men and women from all over the world for partial and full sponsorships. We've also had a record number of riders purchase custom and prototype equipment from our lines solely for the Olympic games," Stephen answered casually.

"Have we gotten any further with the three female riders that you and I spoke about last week?"

"I'm still working on that. They are all locked into contracts with other companies until after the Olympics."

"Alright, let's meet again next week. I want to know exactly what is going on and with whom before I get to Aspen."

"I do believe we're suppose to unveil a brand new

prototype called the *Rapture* in March at the Women's US Open Snowboarding Championships, is that right?" Martie asked.

"Yes. Rory will be in Vermont for that event and the testing on the new board should definitely be completed a few weeks beforehand."

"Well, hopefully we have an American female contracted with us and riding our board at the event. I can't tell you how bad that will look for us if it doesn't happen, Stephen." She eyed him, pursing her lips.

"Other than that, it looks like we're starting our snow season off with a bang guys. I want all of the information on the prototype boards for the X Games and Olympics on my desk by the twenty-eighth of this month—that includes the test documentation as well." She took her glasses off and slid them into the pocket inside her suit jacket.

"Yes ma'am, our test teams are supposed to leave this week. One crew is headed to Stockholm and the other to Aspen. Both groups will be back by the twenty-sixth and our final drafts should be completed by January fourteenth," a redhead with a bouncy ponytail replied.

"Thank you, Johanna. As head of our testing department, it's up to you to make sure everything runs smoothly. We'll meet again when you've returned with some results for me. As for everyone else, this is it, this is where we make it or break it. This is our first trip as a corporation to either of these events, and we're pushing to be the lead equipment sponsor, so I'm putting it all on you guys to make sure we're definitely invited back, and as always, above everything else, the main factor here is our boards. Let's do everything we can to make sure our boards come off the line number one and stay there. I would expect that each and every one of you has the same pride in this company that I do. There is a reason why riders in other countries are calling on us to purchase equipment. Let's make sure we pursue the top riders in all fields. The more people that are seen riding our boards and using our equipment at these upcoming events will directly affect our retail sales. Keep that in mind."

Rory stood up, grabbing the files that were handed to her from Stephen and Johanna before exiting the room. Martie stayed behind to have a smaller meeting with Stephen, Johanna, and a few of the top designers.

~ ~ ~

"Rory, I'm stepping out for lunch. Would you like me to pick you up anything?"

"Oh no, Alex, I'm fine. Thanks for asking. You might want to see if Martie wants anything. I haven't talked to her since the meeting this morning. You usually eat lunch early. Are you feeling ok?"

"Yes ma'am. I'm just running some personal errands today, so I decided to do it later. I spoke with Martie briefly about an hour ago and she said she'd pick something up."

"Ok, well, have a nice lunch."

Rory dialed Martie's extension leaving a voicemail when she didn't answer. She headed down to the second floor to take a look at some of the new snowboard and surfboard prototypes that were being manufactured. Usually, Martie accompanied her, but she had gone alone since Martie was obviously out of her office. She'd been on the production floor for nearly an hour when her cell phone rang.

"Hey, where are you?" she answered.

"I'm on my way down," Martie said." I just got back from having lunch with a guy that you'll remember very well. He's now working for Extreme boards, in your old position."

"Oh, how nice. You had lunch with one of our rivals and my old employer. I hope I'm not paying you to help out the competition, Martina!"

"Come on, Rory. You know better than that. I'm as loyal to you as a dog. He called me to see how you were doing and he wanted to get together and talk for old times' sake. Nothing really to do with work."

"Ok, you've got me. I could really care less what you do on your lunch break, mate, but I'm sure you want me to ask who it was that you were talking to. I guess I'm a little curious. So, who was it and what did they want?"

As soon as she paused, the line went dead. *Oh how cute, Martie. Lead a thirsty horse to an empty trough. You're such a pain in my ass. Some best friend you are.* Rory spun on her heels to walk back to the elevator.

"There you are. I hung up when I saw you," Martie said, greeting her.

Rory shook her and smiled.

"So, I had lunch with Stewart Gunner. You remember him right? He won the Men's WCT in 2013. We used to—"

"Yes, I know who he is. Why is he bothering you?" Rory asked.

"He just moved here and isn't surfing the pro tour anymore. He said he got my name from a friend. Who knows? Anyway, he sure hasn't changed much."

"Ok anymore blasts from the past up your sleeve

18

today? I'm really not in the mood for a stroll down memory lane ok, Martie? We have a hundred things that need to be done before next month. None of them include surfing. This is our snow season. Oh, I almost forgot, you need to make sure you send a representative to the Roxy Pro in Australia next month. After that there is nothing on the surf calendar until March. So send someone to make sure our riders are on our boards at the event. Then, I don't want to hear the word surfing until after the Olympics."

"Yes ma'am, Captain." Martie threw up a mock salute and Rory shot her a go to hell look from her ice cold baby blue eyes.

"Come on, I'm almost finished. I have one more person to visit and then I'm going to step out for about two hours and grab some lunch."

"While you're out, call Angel. I'm sure she'd like to hear from you today, especially since you're sending someone to Australia in your place next month."

~ ~ ~

Rory hadn't noticed the time flying by, until Alex knocked on the door to say she was heading home. It was six-thirty and most of the office staff and design staff had gone for the day. Martie had been on her way out behind Alex. She'd stopped to check Rory's office and sure enough she was typing away at her computer and had just hung up the phone.

"Come on, Rory. Let's get out of here. You've been here all day. I'm sure you're ready to go home and relax

19

or at least eat something. I bet you skipped lunch while you were out, didn't you?"

"I'm fine, mate and I have a lot of work to do still."

"Damn it, Rory, working seventy hours a week is ridiculous. You shouldn't be working like a dog, especially today. You're not the only one with deadlines and piles of work to do. Let's go have a drink or something."

"No, and today of all days, I'm fine! How many times do I have to tell you, Martina? I'm fine. Okay? I've moved on with my life. The past is the past! Now if you would please excuse me, I have things that I need to get finished before I leave."

"Alright, if you want to act like an ass, go ahead, but don't you come running to me when it catches up to you, and trust me, Rory Eden, it will catch your ass one day!"

Martie slammed the door and walked down to the elevator. Being best friends with Rory was one of the hardest things she'd ever done. She had to sit back and watch a woman that she loved like a sister, throw her life away over a near fatal accident. She hurt inside almost as equally as Rory did, yet she couldn't understand why Rory had never faced what had happened to her. She slowly recovered and had gone to work a year later, never surfing again. The only time she'd ever spoken about surfing was for work purposes. Four years had gone by and Rory had suffered inside every day. No one saw it except for Martie because she saw right through the façade.

~ ~ ~

Rory drove her Audi through the iron gates, up the

driveway and into the garage, just after eight p.m. She got out, carrying her briefcase and cell phone as she walked into the house, setting them both in the study, before walking upstairs to her bedroom.

Ten minutes later, Rory stood in the sand on the beach behind her house, wearing a sports bra under her sweat shirt and a loose pair of warm-up pants. Her feet were bare in the cold, wet sand. She started the slow motion of Tai Chi, moving her body in rhythm, gracefully from one stance to the next. The full moon cast a shadow behind her, mimicking her every action. It was a clear California night, with stars blanketing the ocean as far as the eye could see. It was an absolutely perfect night for most people, but not Rory. Her body moved through the motions as her mind played back the painful memories and her heart felt the sadness of her loss.

An hour later, she sat down in the sand, listening to the waves crashing against the shore as a few tears fell. The beautiful scenery reminded her of a time when she had been happy. A time when no matter what day it was, as soon as she'd seen the sky, smelled the salt of the ocean and heard the waves crashing, she'd been happy. That happiness had died with her on that beach in Hawaii and it hadn't been resuscitated with her in the hospital.

Back inside, she poured herself a glass of whiskey, sipping it on her way up the winding staircase to her bedroom. She showered off the salty sweat and tears, finishing her glass before crawling between the sheets and forcing herself to forget for another year.

Chapter Two

Two weeks had gone by since Rory had faced the anniversary of her accident. She'd trained herself to focus further away from it every year as it passed. Nothing seemed to change her routine. Christmas also passed right by. Rory had spent Christmas Eve and Christmas Day at Martie's. They'd exchanged a few gifts and watched old movies.

Rory fell right back into her work routine Monday morning as she awoke at four a.m. to the buzzing of the alarm. Knowing she had to get up, she slowly slid out from under the covers and into warm-up pants and a sports bra. Outside on the beach, she went through a short Tai Chi routine to wake up her muscles and stretch out, before taking off in a jog. She always returned to the house, galloping like she was a champion sprinter. This had been the only thing that still made her feel alive; that and the hot steamy shower that usually followed.

Rory made her way downstairs, stopping in the

kitchen. She hadn't realized she still needed to go to the grocery store. Luckily, she still had a half gallon of fat free milk, so she poured herself a small glass and drank it while she buttered a plain piece of toast. *I really need to go to the store. This is crazy. One morning, I'm going to wake up and have to stop at Mc Donald's for breakfast.* She cringed.

~ ~ ~

The tiny convertible Audi with the license plate-BRN2SRF looked like a black streak as it turned the corner into the parking garage for her office building. Rory stepped out, shuffling her briefcase to her right hand and scrambling to answer her ringing cell phone.

"Rory Eden."

"Hi, Rory. This is Carl Farmer with security. I'm calling to make you aware of an early morning visitor. A young woman has been trying to contact you for approximately a week now and it appears as though she has somehow entered the building. I'm sending a guard to escort you inside."

"Carl, I've told you a hundred times I'm not a child and I don't need a personal security escort to enter my own company. When you find the girl, tell her I'm tied up in meetings all day and leave it at that." *Whoever this girl is, she must be very hard up for a sponsorship, either that or a washed up autograph, neither of which she will get.*

Rory ended the call and entered the doors on the first floor of the building in time to see a young blond being escorted out of the side door emergency exit.

"Wait! Wait! Let go of me you asshole! Miss Eden!

Can I speak to you please? It's very important!"

"I'm not sure what you want, but I stopped signing autographs four years ago. A representative will speak to you if you'd like," Rory said, ignoring the girl as she stepped into the elevator.

On the top floor, the doors swung open and Alex was standing there with Martie. Both women looked as though 9/11 had happened once again.

"What? Why the hell are you two staring at me like that? Did I forget to put something on?"

"Did you see her down there? Carl said there was a girl in the building searching for you. How close did she get? Are you ok?" Alex asked.

"Rory, I had no idea she was in the building. Carl told me you wanted a rep to speak to her, so I sent Lisa down there. I didn't know she was coming after you. My God, the nerve of that girl. She'll be lucky if she doesn't get arrested. I swear these kids will do anything for a chance to be famous or in a damn magazine."

"Calm down. Alex, you sound like I was mugged and Martie, do you not remember the hell we went through to get sponsored? Give the girl a break. Yeah she's a little headstrong, but I'm sure she's harmless. Besides, she doesn't even know how things work around here. Talking to me isn't going to help, that's why I wanted a rep to speak with her. If I took the time to personally look at everyone that wanted a chance, I'd never have time to run this company. Everyone back to work, we have deadlines around here people. Chop-chop," Rory said, sidestepping the women on the way to her office at the end of the hall.

~ ~ ~

Rory sat in the overly comfortable executive leather chair behind her desk, taking off her glasses and tossing them on top of the folder sitting next to the computer monitor. She'd attended three meetings with the Snow Team and had held fourteen national and international phone calls. Lunchtime had already come and gone. Martie had stayed at her own desk most of the day, working on her own agenda.

Just as she stood up to stretch, Rory's cell phone rang in its holder on her belt. She looked down at the caller ID and immediately pushed the red button, sending the call to her voicemail. She glanced around her spacious office, her eyes pausing momentarily on the framed magazine covers on the wall. Her name and photo grazed every one of them. Rory took a deep breath, shaking her head slightly and walked out into the hallway.

"Alex, have you seen Martie this afternoon. She hasn't been in my hair since the last meeting this morning. She didn't take off early did she?"

"No ma'am. She's been in her office just as you were. Is there anything I can do for you?"

"Oh no, I'm fine, just stretching my legs. I get tired of staring at those same four walls." She smiled and laughed a little as she started down the hall. She stopped at the closed door a few feet away, knocking softly as she opened it. Martie was turned around, facing the floor to ceiling window and talking on the phone. She quickly spun around in her chair and hung up the phone when she noticed Rory standing in front of her desk.

"What's up, Rory? I figured you were sitting on the floor under your desk, since I haven't heard a peep out of you for um..." She looked down at the silver watch on her right wrist. "It's been almost five hours. Wow, I'm amazed. Honestly, I didn't think..."

"Oh shut up, Martie. I'm just as busy as you are, if not busier, so I don't want to hear your shit. I actually came down here to check out a suspicious notion, and sure enough I was right. How long have you been talking to her, and I don't mean just now?"

"Rory, you know someone has to keep your mother in the loop of your life because you sure as hell don't. If it wasn't for me, she'd have no idea what kind of life her only child was leading, except for what your Uncle Mick tells her or she reads in a magazine. Besides, I needed to tell her you weren't going to the Roxy Pro."

"I don't care to hear the poor pitiful me excuses. It's over Martie. It's been over for four damn years. I've moved on with my life and I wish the rest of you would too. I'm sure she would've noticed that I wasn't there eventually."

"Come on, she's all you have. How long do you plan on shutting her out?"

As long as it hurts, or until the pain stops, whichever comes first! Rory started to speak, but stopped before the words left her mouth. Instead they faded off into her thoughts. Martie stood up and walked around the desk towards Rory. She knew she wouldn't get through to her, not today, but she'd keep her promise to Angel and continued trying to reach deep inside, past the pain, to the part of Rory she knew still existed; the part of her that died four years ago on the beach.

"Have you heard from Carl? Did he get anything out of that girl from this morning?" Martie asked.

"No I guess not, Carl hasn't called me. What about

Lisa, did she find out what she was here for?"

"Nope, the girl took off before Lisa could speak to her. I don't like the smell of this, Rory. Be careful. Who knows who she is or what her motive is for that matter. I don't think she'll be back, but then again she'd been trying for two weeks to get in here and see you. On the lighter side, maybe she has a crush on you. That would be quite funny. I can see it in the next issue of Surf's Up Magazine. 'Rory Eden, retired pro surfer and head of Eden Boards, Inc. the largest surf and snow board design and manufacturing company in the world, is stalked by a love struck teenage girl with a crush.' Man, would that be hilarious!" Martie laughed.

"Laugh it up, mate, I swear. Besides you're probably the one with a crush and as oblivious as I am, I made you my vice president. Go figure!"

"Oh please, woman! You'd know it if I had a crush. Anyway, been there, done that. Don't get me wrong, it was great and I will always love you, but you're way too enigmatic for me. I don't know whether you're coming or going half of the time. Hey, don't you have work to do or something? Can't you see I'm busy here? What happened to 'chop-chop' and 'we have work to do people'?"

Rory laughed at Martie's attempt at blowing right past the discussion of their brief attempt as a couple.

"Fine, I get your point. We lasted all of about two months, but I do believe you were the cause of the break-up. Something about not dating your mates and I was too much like a sister or something along those lines," Rory teased.

Martie's deep brown eyes grew as big as baseballs as she started towards Rory with her hands clenched.

"Okay, I get the hint!" Rory laughed backing away from her friend. "Do me a favor, next time you talk to Angel, tell her I'm too busy to talk. I'd prefer it if you didn't talk to my mum at all, but since you never do what I say or suggest, make sure it's known that I don't want to speak to her," she said seriously, before leaving the room.

~ ~ ~

It was eight o'clock by the time Rory's midnight blue Audi rolled through the iron gates of her property. She parked the car in the garage and walked into her house. She stopped inside the study to turn on her laptop, before strolling up the stairs and into her lavish bedroom with a balcony and an ocean view. She walked into her closet, stripping off her company shirt and chino style pants and tossing them into the overflowing basket full of dirty clothes. She put on a white t-shirt, then slipped a canary yellow polo shirt over it and pulled on a pair of khaki colored cargo pants. She stopped momentarily, looking at herself in the mirror before exiting her room.

Rory walked through the open doorway of her study and sat in the leather chair behind the desk, bumping the wireless mouse next to the laptop to turn off the screensaver. Her personal computer had the same program as the one in her office, so she was able to continue working when she was at home. Rory yawned softly as she ran her fingers through her short blond hair. She logged into her office software and her inbox flashed three new messages. She walked into the living room in search of her iPod when she heard the doorbell on the gate ring. She pressed the call button on the intercom thinking it was Martie trying to redeem herself, even though she knew the code to get in.

"I thought we handled this at the office?" Rory said.

"Rory, I'm sorry for the mess I caused at your company today. If you'd just give me a chance, I only want to talk to you for a minute."

Rory jumped back from the intercom, wondering whether she should call the cops or go out there and confront the girl. *This girl has balls, I'll give her that. Sneaking into my office and now showing up at my home.*

"Look, mate... I really don't have time to speak to you. I can set up an appointment with one of my representatives if you'd like, but I don't handle the recruiting. I'm sorry."

"I would really rather speak directly to you. It won't take long, I promise."

Rory heard another voice in the background as the girl was speaking.

The young blond at the gate turned to her friend who was standing next to her.

"Damn it, Lori, if you don't shut up you're going to blow this for me."

"Look, Austin, you almost got us arrested this morning and now you're really in deep. If she calls the cops, this is stalking and harassment and probably ten other fucking things. Let's get the hell out of here. I don't like this."

"You're such a pussy. Come on we're not going to jail. She's not Cruella De-Ville and besides we're not doing anything wrong. I'm just trying to speak to her."

Neither of them realized that Austin had been holding the intercom button throughout their entire conversation, until Rory came back on the other end.

"Uh… Austin…is that your name? I think you'd better listen to your mate. You were thrown out of my office building and now you're trying to enter my property. If I call the police you will more than likely get arrested for stalking. Look, if you really want to be seen that badly, call my office in the morning and ask to speak to Lisa Keaton. She's one of my surfing reps, I'm assuming you're a surfer right?"

"Yes, uh we both are, but I'd much rather talk to you. I'm not good with the whole corporate ladder thing."

"I can see that, but unfortunately that's the way I work. My reps handle everything until it comes to signing someone, then they see me. If I personally spoke to everyone that thought they deserved a sponsorship, it would take up the rest of my life, and I have a company to run. Now, I'd appreciate it if you'd please remove yourselves from my property and if you're as serious as you seem to be, call my office and speak to Lisa. I'm sure she can help you out. Goodnight."

Rory stood by the intercom, waiting until she no longer heard noise from the two girls, before going back to the study.

~ ~ ~

Rory reached down for her cell phone when she noticed Martie's BMW in the company parking garage. The phone rang before she could dial out.

"Hey, it's Martie. I received an interesting email this morning from Lisa Keaton. I think you should see it."

"I was just about to call you. I'm proud of you, Martie. You've made it to work before me two days this week. I'm impressed."

"This is serious, Rory. That girl that snuck in here yesterday won't give up. Apparently, she sent an email to the company and requested a meeting with Lisa and she also would like a personal meeting with you."

"Yeah, I already know. She stopped by my house last night."

"She did what! Oh my God, Rory! Did you call the cops?" Martie screeched, pacing the floor in the hall waiting for the elevator to stop. One hand was holding her cell phone against her ear and the other was in the pocket of her black pants suit.

"No, I didn't call the cops. Geez, Martie, don't be so paranoid."

"Paranoid! Excuse me. You had a stalker show up at your house in the middle of the night. What am I suppose to think? You didn't let her in the gate did you?"

"No, of course not. I called down to the intercom and told her to speak with Lisa in the morning if she wanted to be looked at by our company because I don't deal directly with prospects. The odd part is, she wasn't alone. I guess the other girl had been with her at the office too."

"I don't like—" Martie was cut off by the elevator opening.

Rory was standing there grinning. Her light colored hair and baby blue eyes stood out in contrast to her bronzed skin. If anyone noticed her impeccable good looks when she was around them, they ignored it. Martie knew firsthand what that was like. She'd had her chance with Rory and chose to be her best friend instead. In her own words, it was safer to love her and have her in her life forever as a best friend than to have her as a lover and lose her to someone or something else down the road.

"I think you can hang up now, Martie, unless of course, I'm imagining you standing there with your jaw on the floor."

Martie grabbed Rory's hand, urging her past Alex and through the door of her office. Once inside, she closed the door and spun around. Rory put her briefcase on the floor and sat down in her chair with hands folded neatly in front of her on the desk.

"How can you sit there looking so calm and smug? I don't get you, I swear I don't. Personally, I would've called the cops and had the damn kid arrested for stalking. What happens when she comes back, as you and I both know she will?"

"Well, if she comes back, I guess I'll have to handle it, now won't I. Honestly, I think it's over with. I explained the way things work last night and she contacted Lisa afterwards, so as far as I can see, it's over with."

"Ok, fine, don't come crawling to me when she kicks your door in or jumps in your car at a red light or some stupid shit like that."

Rory sat back laughing. "Get real, Martie. I seriously doubt anything like that will happen."

Martie shook her head, walking out of the office. She stopped in the hallway, turning back towards the closed door. *Damn it, Rory. You don't see it and it's right in front of you. This girl is wild and reckless just like you were, not too long ago. You've pushed that part of your life and that side of you so far away, that you don't even remember it anymore. The fire in your eyes burned out four years ago.*

Rory picked up her phone, dialing an extension as Martie shut the door. "Hello Lisa, it's Rory," she said

32

when the bubbly woman answered.

"Hello, Rory. How may I help you?"

"A girl contacted you last night or this morning requesting a meeting, correct?"

"Yes ma'am she did. I received an email from her this morning. I've never heard of her though, so I don't think—"

"Martie spoke with me briefly about it. Can you please forward the email to my inbox when you get a chance?"

"Uh, yes ma'am. I'll send it to you right now."

"Thanks, Lisa. By the way, how are things coming along down there?"

"Great, we should have the new prototype board ready to test while you're in Aspen."

"That's awesome! I'm definitely looking forward to seeing it. I talked to Jacob Nettles and Calvin Whittle yesterday about the Roxy Pro in Australia."

"We should have a large portion of the riders on our boards at Roxy."

"Sounds great, Lisa. Oh, one other thing before I forget. If this girl contacts you again, forward the emails to me instead of Martie please."

"Sure, no problem."

"Great, thanks. Have a nice afternoon."

Rory hung up and waited a few minutes before checking her inbox and clicking on the forwarded message.

To: Lisa_Keaton@EdenBoardsInc.com
From: ECSurfergrl@Media.net
Subject: Meeting w/ Rory Eden about Surfing

Lisa Keaton,

My name is Austin Tinsley. I'm trying to meet with Rory Eden. I have something to discuss with her that is personal. It's not just about a surfing sponsorship. I was told to contact you. If you could please forward my information to Rory that would be greatly appreciated. My phone number is 454-8001, and my email address is ECSurfergrl@Media.net. Thank you for your time.

Sincerely,

Austin C. Tinsley

Rory wondered what exactly it was she wanted to discuss so badly. *Personal? What the hell can you possibly want with me? Bloody hell, I don't have time to be a role model or whatever it is she wants.*

~ ~ ~

Before she knew it, it was lunch time and today of all days, Rory decided to join Martie for lunch down at the small café on the corner. Martie parker her black BMW next to the curb and both women walked through the glass doors, sitting at the first available table. An older waitress with a bad dye job came over to them.

"Good afternoon ladies, what can I get for you?"

Martie was the first to answer since she frequently ate at the restaurant. "I'll have a cup of the cream of chicken and mushroom soup, a small garden salad, and water."

"Ok and for you ma'am?" she asked Rory.

"I'll have a cup of the broccoli cheese soup, half of a turkey club, and water also."

The waitress walked away and Martie leaned forward in her seat.

"So what brought your ass out of the office today? You never leave for lunch. I wasn't sure if I should call the newspaper or something!"

"Oh, I don't know. I got tired of staring at my office walls I guess. Why, does it bother you that I wanted to have lunch? You always ask and I always say no. So, I thought what the hell, I'll go today."

"I see. Any word from the kid?"

"No, I told you it was over."

"Uh huh, I'll believe it when I see it. You can't trust people like that."

The waitress returned with their food and both women ate with a passion. One thing that they'd definitely had in common was eating. Both women could put away some food without their bodies ever showing it. They blamed it on having a high metabolism from being athletes for so many years.

"I guess we'd better get back. I have so much to get done this week. Alex said she has all of your travel information ready. I wish I was going with you to this one. Aspen is such a beautiful place."

"Yeah, I'm sure I'll enjoy it."

"Hey, what are you doing for New Year's? Any big dates I should know about?"

"Actually, I do have a date this year." Rory smiled and started laughing when Martie's face scrunched up in shock. "A date with the TV, that is."

"Come on, Rory. It's a weekend this year, so you

have no excuses about having to get up early to go into the office. You're coming out with me here in L.A. since we don't have shit in Long Beach. Remind me again why we both bought houses out there."

"Beach, duh!" Rory put major emphasis on the word beach as she smiled at Martie.

"Yeah, you're right I couldn't possibly live inland. We'll pick you up around seven Saturday night."

"We?"

"Yeah, me and the black stretched limo."

"I see, and where are we going? I've been invited to so many New Year's parties. I wouldn't know where to begin."

Both women tossed cash on the table to cover the bill, continuing their conversation as they stood up. Neither of them noticed Austin walking by on the sidewalk as they exited the café. Austin immediately noticed Rory and she quickly moved towards her. Martie saw the girl approaching before Rory and instantaneously reached for her cell phone to call the police.

"Excuse me, Rory. I'm the one that was at your house last night as well as in your office building," she said, pulling her dark aviator sunglasses off.

Rory studied the young girl for a moment. She was shorter than Rory by a couple of inches and definitely in shape. Sun-kissed skin stood out next to the white t-shirt that clung to her in the right places and she wore shorts that hung slightly off her hips. She had long, naturally wavy, dark blond hair that was pulled back up off her neck in a clip, accentuating her beautiful gray eyes. Rory couldn't peel her eyes away. She heard Martie talking and turned to see another girl, about an inch taller with a similar build, with short dark hair and brown eyes.

"Martie, hang up the phone. There's no need to call the cops."

Martie didn't hesitate as she moved towards the girls, still holding her phone.

"Look, I suggest you both stay as far away as you can from Rory. She doesn't handle whatever it is you're looking for. You've contacted a representative from our company and that's as far as you need to go. If you're seen anywhere near our building or Rory's private residence again, I will personally make sure you both go to jail for stalking. Do you understand me? I'm dead serious. This is not a game anymore."

"I'm sorry if we upset anyone, we were just trying to speak to Rory. We're not stalking anyone."

"Excuse me! You snuck into our building and you—"

"Okay, Martie, I think they get the point. There's no need to scare the hell out of them. Come on I have a meeting in an hour."

Both women walked briskly towards the BMW. Rory turned back towards the girls as she was getting into the car.

"Listen, mate, I understand where you're coming from. Unfortunately, I can't help you. I'm not the person you need to be speaking with. Please understand how my company works." *I wish I could help you, but I'm sorry, I can't.*

Chapter Three

Rory walked out of her bedroom wearing black pants, a white button down blouse with a light gray V-neck sweater over it and black Doc Marten's. She sat on the couch in her living room watching a New Year's Eve Celebration show on the TV. Ten minutes later, she heard the bell ring for the gate. She grabbed her leather jacket and walked outside, locking the door before turning around. The driver, who was dressed in a tuxedo, had the door opened, waiting for her as she walked down the driveway.

"Good evening, Miss Eden. My name is John," he said as she punched the numbers for the code to open and then close the gate.

"It's nice to meet you, John."

"Likewise."

Rory slid into the car and John shut the door. Martie was sitting across from her, wearing black pants, a crème colored turtle neck, and black zip up ankle boots. She also had a black leather jacket with her. Martie leaned over, pouring two glasses of champagne as the car drove away. She took one glass, handing the other to Rory.

"Here's to a New Year with good health and a future full of snow covered mountains and double overhead waves!" Martie leaned forward with her glass.

"I can definitely drink to that! Cheers, mate!" Rory leaned in and tapped her glass against Martie's.

~ ~ ~

The limo pulled up in front of the twelve story Palace Hotel and both women exited the car when John opened the door. Martie turned back towards him.

"I'll call you when we're ready to go. I don't see a need for you to hang around in the lot, unless of course you want to. It's up to you."

"Thank you, Martie. I'll be right outside when you're ready to leave."

Both women walked into the hotel and Martie directed Rory over to the elevator, handing the attendant her invitation. He took them up to the penthouse floor. Rory had no idea what party it was until the elevator doors opened and she saw the sign by the penthouse entrance doors. The party was being held by 'On The Edge', a surfing and snowboarding magazine out of Los Angeles.

"I thought we were going to a bar."

"We got a last minute invitation," Martie shrugged.

As Rory and Martie made their way into the party and towards the bar, they ran into a few familiar faces from the surfing and snowboarding network of people that were their business acquaintances. The full liquor bar ran along one of the side walls. Martie ordered a dirty martini and Rory ordered a whiskey. Just as Rory was handed her drink, the magazine editor greeted them.

"Hello, Rory and Martie. I'm Frank Wright, editor of On The Edge Magazine. Thank you both for coming. We're happy you could make it."

"Thanks. If you will excuse us, I see someone I want to introduce Rory to," Martie said, pulling Rory away. "That man's a scumbag. I heard he's banged just about every employee, male and female," Martie muttered.

Rory cringed. "Gross."

Martie walked over to a group of women standing near the window, talking. A few of the women recognized Rory and Martie immediately from articles that they'd written.

Rory and Martie introduced themselves to the writers that they didn't know.

"How's business going, ladies?" A tall brunette named Carina asked. Rory acted nonchalant as she sarcastically answered back.

"Well, being as how we're coming into snow season with surf season around the corner I'd say business is on the launch pad waiting to be fueled."

Martie laughed, loving her best friend's odd sense of humor. A few of the other women chuckled as well.

Carina eyed her suspiciously, but Rory simply shrugged and walked away. She'd never been a fan of the cat and mouse game and hooking up with some random person wasn't her style.

~ ~ ~

Two and half hours later, Martie and Rory were both ready to ditch the party. They'd both had enough entertainment to last at least six months. Martie called John, who was readily available and waiting for them outside. After the half-hour drive back to Long Beach, Rory decided she was ready to call it a night. John dropped her off at home and Martie went on to another party.

Rory walked inside, tossing her jacket on the couch as she moved into the kitchen. She grabbed a beer out of the refrigerator, kicked her shoes off, rolled the bottom of her pants up a bit and put on her flip flops, before walking through the French doors and out onto the pool deck. She opened the beer bottle as she opened the gate and slipped through the dunes, down into the cool sand near the water. She didn't have a destination in mind as she walked a little ways, drinking her beer and listening to the waves crashing against the shore.

About a half a mile and a quarter of a bottle later, she walked past someone sitting in the sand near the dunes. At first she paid no attention to the person, until the moonlight lit up her face and she realized it was Austin, the young girl that had been trying to contact her. *Oh bloody hell. I really don't need you right now. Damn it, Rory, you idiot, you just had to go for a walk didn't you? But this is a private beach she's sitting on. Hmm... at least she's not on my property. Oh well.* Rory kept walking and finally came to a stop when she heard her name being called. Austin jogged slightly, catching up with the woman who had once been dubbed the queen of surf.

"Hello, Rory. I wasn't expecting to see you out on

New Year's Eve."

"Yeah well I wasn't expecting to see you out on my beach at eleven thirty at night either."

"Touché."

"Look, mate. I'm not really in the mood for a stalking session or whatever this is ok."

"Actually, I'd just like to walk with you if you don't mind."

"You don't give up do you?" Rory sighed.

Austin grinned.

Rory walked away, drinking her lager and Austin fell into step next to her. They walked in silence, listening to the soft crash of the waves against the shore as the moon lit their path. Five minutes later, Austin spoke softly.

"I used to watch you on TV and I bought every magazine that you were in."

Rory kept walking quietly, wishing she'd poured herself a whiskey instead of opting for a beer.

"I admire you as much now as I did then. You inspired me to follow my dreams. You used to surf with such skill and determination. You were the best in the world, one with the ocean, and then all of a sudden it was ripped right out from under you."

Rory stopped suddenly, turning towards the young woman at her side.

"What's in the past stays in the past. I don't live my life around the past and neither should you. Now if you don't mind, I'd prefer to walk along thinking about the future. It's New Year's Eve, mate!"

Austin started laughing, which only pissed Rory off even more.

"What the bloody hell are you laughing at?"

"Well your accent must come out heavier when

you're mad or drinking, but either way, it's cute. I almost forgot you were from Australia. I guess I've never really heard you talk much, though. The accent sounds a little funny coming from you, but it's...I like it."

Rory hadn't even realized her accent had surfaced, thicker than ever. It generally only ever came out when she was back in Australia or too upset to think about what she was saying. She calmed down slightly before speaking again.

"Look, whoever you are, I'm not in the mood to discuss things that happened a long time ago..."

"Rory, I really didn't mean to upset you, honestly. I was only being truthful and trying to make small talk. Here let me start over." Austin stuck her right hand out. "Hi, I'm Austin Tinsley. It's nice to meet you. Once upon a time, I was a huge fan of yours and still am to this day, but that's not the reason that I'm here talking to you."

"Okay, Miss Tinsley. You've been trying for weeks to get my attention and now you have it. Five minutes is all I can spare," Rory said.

Austin noticed the New Year had arrived, looking down at her watch. It was two minutes after twelve. She threw caution to the wind.

"Rory, it's midnight and it's bad luck to ring in the New Year without a kiss," she said quickly, stepping up close to Rory and pressing her lips against Rory's. The kiss lasted a mere second before Rory backed away with a shocked expression on her face.

"Excuse me, what the hell do you think you're doing?"

"Ringing in the New Year with good luck." Austin smiled.

Rory could hardly stand still. She wasn't sure what to do. Her lips tingled and her heart raced and the girl standing in front of her barely looked old enough to be legal. *Oh My God, Rory. You have to set this kid straight, right now!*

"Look, Miss Tinsley, I uh...well this is...shit...ok, listen, mate. I'm a lot older than you and this crush you have is never going to work. So..."

Austin couldn't contain the laughter as she watched Rory struggle with her words, trying not to use her buried accent.

"Please call me Austin and although I am most definitely old enough, I'm not looking to sleep with you. I just believe in good luck that's all. I'm not pursuing you to have a sexual affair, alright."

"Well, that's certainly nice to know. So, Austin, why *are* you pursuing me?"

"Rory, like I've said before, I'm a huge fan and always have been. I'm a surfer myself and I'd really like to get to know you. I want to learn everything you know. I want to be a pro surfer and I want you to teach me everything you know and train me so I can join the tour."

Rory started walking in the direction of her house. She stayed quiet for about five minutes. Austin strolled along next to her. This had been the last thing she'd expected the young woman to say.

"Okay, so let me get this straight. You've been stalking me because you want me to be your trainer?"

"Well, I haven't been stalking you, just sort of trying to get your attention."

"Right, well, in my world that's stalking, but that's neither here nor there." Rory burst out laughing. "You're serious aren't you?"

Austin stopped walking and starred at Rory with a determined look on her face.

"Of course I'm serious. I moved from the East Coast so that I could have good waves and a better opportunity. You're by far the best of the best and who better to help me."

"I haven't had anything to do with surfing in over four years. What can I possible do to help you?"

"Come on, Rory, it's like riding a bike, you never forget it and you know it."

"Yeah, well this old horse has been rode hard and put up dry. I'm afraid she *has* forgotten….everything." Rory took the last sip of her lager and began walking again. She started up the path through the dunes to her house. Austin stopped at the beginning of the dunes. Well aware that she was on Rory's private property.

"By the way, I'm twenty-one. I'm an adult, not some little kid like you seem to think."

Rory answered back. "Yeah well, I'm not Australian like you seem to think. I'm American. I was born in California. As for the accent, my mother is Australian and I spent most of my childhood on the Gold Coast, so I guess you could say I picked up the native slang."

Just before Rory entered her house, Austin spoke once more.

"Rory, I'm only asking you to give it some thought. Just toss around the idea. Please?"

Rory turned back towards the darkness where she knew Austin was standing.

"Miss Tinsley, the answer is as it always will be, no. Happy New Year."

Rory walked inside, locking the door behind her.

Austin Tinsley, you're one very headstrong young woman. Life's not always perfect sets and double overhead waves. One day you'll learn that. I just hope I'm not the one that has to teach it to you.

Chapter Four

New Year's weekend had passed and on Monday morning, Rory's blue Audi bolted through the streets of Long Beach and onto the highway. Thirty minutes later, she sped into the parking garage for her office building with the convertible top down and loud music blaring on the radio. Martie arrived shortly after, catching up to Rory as they entered the main doors.

"You look good today. The gray shirt contrasts nicely with those gorgeous eyes of yours."

"Stop trying to flirt, Martie. It's not going to get you anywhere." Rory smiled as she stepped into the elevator.

"I'm not flirting, smart ass. I was giving you a compliment. So anyway, how did the rest of your night go? We dropped you off way too early!"

"Well, I'd tell you, but you'd never believe it, so let's just say I spent a quiet night out on the beach."

"Wouldn't believe it? You couldn't possibly have hooked up with anyone. Number one, that's not you and number two, you live around a bunch of rich old people."

47

Rory was laughing as the elevator doors opened to their floor. Alex was sitting at her desk. When Rory had first hired her, Martie had bet Rory that she'd never last and Alex had surprised them both. She'd turned out to be the most punctual person in the entire building.

"Good morning, ladies. It certainly sounds like you're enjoying the New Year. Everything must have gotten off to a great start for you."

"Yes, well it's another year so what the hell, right?" Rory replied.

Rory sat down at her desk and turned her computer on. She smiled when she noticed the email at the top of her inbox.

TO: R_Eden@EdenBoardsInc.com
From: ECSurfergrl@Media.net
Subject: Some thought

Rory,

I'm very serious about our conversation. I'm willing to do whatever it takes. Please give it some serious thought before you completely make a decision. I understand you're very busy with your company. I'm not asking for an arm or a leg, just your brain and whatever you decide to throw in with it. I'm not even sure I can afford this, but I'm willing to do everything I can.

Sincerely,

A.C. Tinsley

Rory laughed slightly as she read it. Still unsure whether she should reply or not, she simply clicked the reply later button. There was no way she could devote her time and attention to training someone; much less a surfer. She'd vowed the day she finished her physical therapy that she would never surf again. The only reason she stayed in the industry was because surfing would always be her life and she'd been able to put her college degree and years of surfing knowledge to use when she'd started her own company.

~ ~ ~

At three o'clock that afternoon, Martie walked into Rory's office. Rory took off her glasses and slid the paperwork she had been reading to the side as she leaned back in her chair.

"What's up, Martie?"

"Spill it. You've been acting a little weird today and I'm starting to worry about you. What exactly did you do after the limo dropped you off Saturday night?" Martie asked, sitting in the chair across from her.

Rory smiled and couldn't contain the laughter any longer knowing the suspense was killing Martie.

"Nothing happened really. I walked on the beach and drank a beer. Then I went to bed."

"Somehow I just don't believe you."

"I ran into my stalker. We had…"

"Oh my God, Rory. Did you call the cops? Where was she? I swear I've had it with this kid!"

"Calm down, Martie, she's okay. We actually just talked for a little bit when she walked the beach with me.

Her name's Austin Tinsley."

"Great you're making friends with her now. What's next…you didn't…Rory, tell me you didn't let her in your house."

Rory couldn't stop laughing at Martie's ridiculous behavior.

"No, I didn't invite her inside. We talked briefly and that's it."

"So what exactly did you talk about?"

"Not much, she's a lifelong fan and a diehard surfer. She wants me to teach her everything I know and train her to join the pro tour. That's why she's been so adamant about talking to me."

"What the fuck?"

"I know, weird huh?"

"Well you're not actually considering it, are you?"

"No, of course not. Martie, a little common sense would be good here. If I don't surf anymore, what the hell makes you think I'm going to devote my time to teaching and training someone? I'm about to begin traveling every week for upcoming events. I don't have the time or the energy, and I sure as hell don't want anything to do with my past. I explained to her that I'm in the business end of things now and history is history and it's going to stay history for a reason."

"What if she doesn't give up?"

"Yeah well, I already know she won't," Rory sighed.

Martie looked at all of the framed magazine covers and articles on Rory's wall. She'd graced the cover of a magazine at least thirty times and had had numerous articles written about her. Martie missed that side of Rory, the passionate, yet overtly dangerous wild side. *This girl is just like you Rory, and you don't even see it.*

Unfortunately, she knows how to push your buttons and eventually she'll go beyond the tough skin you hide under. I can't let her hurt you; she doesn't know anything about the terrible pain you've forced yourself to forget about.

"Earth to Martie, hello?"

"What!"

"You zoned out on me, girl. I was about to slap you or something."

"Has she tried to contact you anymore here at the office?"

"As a matter of fact, she emailed me this morning."

"Surely you're not going to respond, right?"

"I don't know, I feel bad for her. I mean there is no way I can do what she's asking of me, but I can at least try to maybe help her find someone who's willing to teach and train her."

"Yeah, well, as long as it's not you. Look, be careful, Rory. You don't know much about this girl." *Besides, she's not going to work with anyone else, it's you she chose and she's not going to stop until she gets what she wants. Your fire burned that deep, a long time ago. Unfortunately, it burned out way too soon.*

"I need to go over a few things with the snow team about Aspen. We still haven't gotten anywhere with the riders that are under contract, unless you want to buy out their contracts."

"No, we're not in that position. I actually took a look at Adler Troy's contract, but it's pretty cut and dry and they want millions to release her. So, I guess we will see how things shake down while I'm there. Who knows, maybe we will get lucky."

"Yeah, she's the top dog. They're not going to let her

go for free, that's for sure. Hey, if you don't mind, I'm going to take off early today. I have a doctor's appointment. Damn yearly check up shit," Martie huffed.

"Aw poor Martie has to get poked by a mean ol' gyno. Why don't you just tell them you're a lesbian? That would make it so much easier, on both of you."

"I have told him. He's just a dirty old man and likes to crack jokes while he's working, if you get my drift."

"Yeah well have a good time. I'll see you in the morning."

"Sure, I so look forward to this every year. Oh and Rory…be careful, if not for me, then for yourself. It's been a long time since you've opened up to anyone. I don't want to see you get hurt. I do care about you, you know."

"I know, I know. It's not like I'm sleeping with her. She's just a baby. I promise not to get in over my head. You know me better than anyone, so you definitely know there's not a Sheila's chance of growing a donger that I'll work with her, much less get close to her."

Martie laughed at Rory's Aussie slang. That was definitely one thing she really missed. Rory used to bounce between American English and Australian English when she spoke. Most of the Aussie slang had worn off since she lived her live permanently in California.

"If I didn't know any better, I'd think it was your Uncle Mick talking just now. My God, Rory, you sounded just like him and no I don't think any women I know are planning on growing a penis as far as I know, so I guess there's no chance that you'll be training her then."

"That would be correct." Rory grinned.

"Well that's good to hear. I'm headed out of here. Have a good rest of your day. I'll see you bright and early, if I can walk."

"Ha-ha, bye."

After Martie shut the door, Rory put her glasses on and went back to her paperwork. When she was finally ready to call it a night and go home, she decided to respond to the email that had been on the back of her mind all day.

TO: ECSurfergrl@Media.net
FROM: R_Eden@EdenBoardsInc.com
Subject: Still thinking…no!

Miss Tinsley,

As I'm sure you're aware, money is not an option. If it were that easy, I would've already discussed this with you. However, at this moment, my schedule is completely booked up and I no longer have anything to do with surfing besides business. Therefore, these both justify my original answer, which is no. I do not see any reason at this time to reconsider. I'm glad you're not looking for arms and legs, since I don't have any extras to spare. As for my brain…I'm sorry but my corporation needs it more than I do. In spite of my lack of availability to assist you, I'm willing to aid you in finding someone with the time and capability to put forth the effort to instruct and prepare you to follow your goals.

Sincerely,

R. Eden

"Well this should set you straight, Miss Tinsley." Rory pressed send and turned off the computer.

~ ~ ~

Three nights later, a Yanni CD played on the outside speakers of the pool deck as Rory stood in the sand between the dunes behind her house, slowly moving through the relaxing motions of her favorite form of Tai Chi. The combination of New Age Inspirational music and ocean waves crashing ashore, helped calm her mind as the Tai Chi routines worked together to relax her body. She found this to be the most peaceful form of self meditation, next to surfing. Back when she had surfed everyday from sunrise to sunset, she'd always found the time for her Tai Chi meditations. In her opinion, this was the best way to clear the human mind. She'd always had her best thoughts during this time. Rory knew in the back of her mind that the waves still called out to her as she stood there in the sand, meditating and exercising. When she had given up her gifted art and love of surfing, she'd sworn to herself that she'd never leave her second art, Tai Chi, for this was the only thing she had left. This was the one thing in her life that couldn't betray her.

Rory went inside after the CD ended, heading straight up the stairs, tossing her sweaty clothes on the way to the shower. She stood under the hot spray cascading from the double showerheads, rinsing the salt from her skin, before soaping off and washing her hair. When she finished, she pulled on an old t-shirt with a surfing logo on it and black cotton warm-up pants and went down to the study, turning on her laptop. Her inbox from the office had mail in it, as usual. She scanned the names until she found the one she knew would be there. She wasn't exactly sure why the young surfer intrigued her, maybe it was because she reminded her of herself. Or, maybe it was simple because Austin Tinsley stirred something in her that she had thought was dead and gone. Clicking on the name staring back at her, she sat back in her leather chair and sighed.

To: R_Eden@EdenBoardsInc.com
From: ECSurfergrl@Media.net
Subject: thinking too hard

Rory,

I would never want to interfere with your corporation. I do know you're a very busy woman. I am, however, asking for a little bit of your spare time. Not a business deal, but more of a friendly agreement. I'd like to get to know you and let you get to know me. Then, maybe you'll understand a little more about where I'm coming from. In the least, please take the time to watch me surf. If you don't like what you see, and you think I stink, well then, I'll forget all about ever asking you for anything. I won't make a fool out of you. That I can promise. I think this a pretty agreeable compromise. Yes?

Sincerely,

A.C. Tinsley

"Damn you're hardheaded. You think you've won, but the game hasn't even begun," Rory said, shaking her head. *I'll reply later, why not make you sweat a little?!*

~ ~ ~

Rory arrived at the office earlier than normal on Friday morning. There were three weeks until the X Games in Aspen and one week away from the Roxy Pro qualifying event in Victoria, Australia. Shockingly, Martie was already in her office. Alex, who was usually the first person from the administration floor to enter the office, wasn't even in the building yet. Rory walked straight into her office and turned on her computer. Before she had a chance to open her inbox, Martie burst through the doors.

"Good Morning sunshine!"

"What's up, Martie? This isn't like you?"

"What's that supposed to mean? Grouch! I can't be in a good mood? Besides, it's Friday."

"Yeah, I know it's Friday. I leave for Aspen in three weeks."

"Speaking of events, who do you want to send to Australia for the Roxy Pro next weekend?"

"I don't care. I left it up to you. It's only a qualifier, so we just need to represent our company. I believe Lisa has a list of our riders that will attend. I know she handles all of our US events, but she knows who'll be there. I met with Katie Phillips, she's our newest rider. Leann Strong is her rep. They were here last week talking with Ian about the new board she's riding."

"Five seven, medium-short brown hair. I met her a few weeks ago. Very cute!"

"My God, Martie, she's like eighteen. Plus, I would bet you my bank account that she's straight."

Martie laughed with an ear to ear smile. "Okay, so I can't take her out on the town with me, she's still legal, and I prefer the straight ones."

"New subject please."

"Hey, didn't we send Greg Underwood to Hawaii last month?"

"Yeah. I was thinking, go ahead and send Leann to the Roxy Pro. That way she can rep the company as well as Kelsey. I believe this girl's going to give Stacey Holbritton a run for her title this season. I think we should go ahead and let Leann handled all of the women's events. Send Greg to everything else. Make sure Lisa covers all of our events here in the states though."

"That sounds good. I'll meet with them this morning and make sure everyone is up to speed on the changes."

"Great, oh and one more thing, Martie, stop chasing our riders. I'm waiting for the day I receive a letter from an attorney regarding you and you're cradle robbing! Dating young straight girls is going to bite you in the ass one day!"

Martie walked away laughing.

Rory realized it was nearly eight and Alex should've arrived. She pressed the button on the intercom.

"Yes, Rory?"

"Good Morning, Alex. When you get a minute, I need to go over my travel arrangements with you. Also, I've made some changes to our traveling representatives. I need to go over that with you as well."

"Yes ma'am. I'll be there in ten minutes."

"Great, thank you."

Alex walked into the office and sat down in front of Rory's desk. They briefly discussed the changes in the schedules, and then quickly talked about the flight and hotel arrangements for Rory's trip to Aspen.

~ ~ ~

Rory closed the program file she was working on, leaning back in her desk chair. Looking down at the watch on her wrist, she was surprised to see what time it was. *Damn, where has this day gone? It's after six. I guess this is as good a time as any.* She clicked on her outbox to send an email.

To: ECSurfergrl@Media.net
From: R_Eden@EdenBoardsInc.com
Subject: answer is still no

Miss Tinsley,

In the corporate world, there is no such thing as 'spare-time'. I spend the majority of my time traveling, as I'm sure you're well aware of. However, you do drive a hard bargain with your 'friendly agreement'. I usually don't see our riders surf or snowboard until after they're already signed with us. I have representatives that watch the trials and preliminaries, and they make the decision to sign the riders that impress them with natural talent and ability. I know this isn't what you want to hear, but unfortunately, it's all I have to offer you at this time. I'm not on much of a personal level with many of my riders.

No offense, I can tell you're a very nice person and I'm sure you're a great surfer. This is simply the way I run my company. I would be very happy to hear that one of my reps has signed you with us. I can definitely see that happening. You have the determination to take you to the top.

Sincerely,

R. Eden

After she sent the email, Rory turned off the computer and locked up her office on her way out. She stopped to say goodnight to Carl before she walking over to the parking garage.

~ ~ ~

Rory noticed the light blinking, indicating a message on the phone as she walked into her home office. Ignoring it, she went upstairs to her bedroom and changed into a white t-shirt with a sports bra underneath and black warm-up pants. After a few light stretches, she went methodically through her Tai Chi routine and then took a long jog down the beach, running as fast as she could on the return back to her house.

She still felt uneasy about the email she had sent to Austin and couldn't get it off her mind as she stood in the shower. Even after reading over it twice, she realized she had come off a little harsh, but she'd had to be honest with the girl. After finishing her shower, she dressed in a t-shirt and shorts, remembering the message on the machine as she made her way back downstairs.

"Hey, it's Martie. I figured you'd be home by now, it's after nine. Damn you work way too much. I was just calling to see if you were watching ESPN. They were talking about the Roxy qualifier that's coming up and mentioned the company. Nothing major, I was just wondering if you were watching, but silly me, you don't have time for television. You're probably out running on the beach or something else less appealing. I'll see you in the morning. Have a good night."

Rory laughed and erased the message. *Martie, I don't know what's more surprising, the fact that I was working late or the fact you're actually home watching TV. You must be looking for a new cradle to prey on.*

Rory stared at her laptop. She had a feeling there was an email awaiting her, but she wasn't sure if she wanted to see it. Sighing, she sat down and turned the computer on. Austin's name was highlighted at the top of her inbox as the most recent incoming message.

To: R_Eden@EdenBoardsInc.com
From: ECSurfergrl@Media.net
Subject: not a contract

Rory,

I know how your company works. I talked to Lisa Keaton as you suggested, however, I do not want Miss Keaton's attention or her acceptance. As I told you in a previous conversation, I admire you. I have always been a huge fan of yours and I'm deeply inspired by you and your surfing style. I want to be your protégé so to speak.

It's your personal approval that I'm looking for, not your company's endorsement. I hope this helps to clear up any confusion about my request.

Sincerely,

A.C. Tinsley

What the hell am I going to do with you? I'm deeply flattered, but...oh, Austin, you poor girl, I'm washed up. There's nothing I could teach that you probably don't already know. You have more drive and ambition than anyone I have ever seen. You deserve a chance, and if this is your only way, well I guess I don't know how else to help you. Rory thought as she clicked the reply button.

To: ECSurfegrl@Media.net
From: R_Eden@EdenBoardsInc.com
Subject: not an agreement either

Miss Tinsley,

Be at Redondo Beach at medium tide tomorrow morning. Meet me in front of Charthouse Restaurant. I'm sure you've surfed there before. That spot has large lefts breaking off the north side of the harbor. We should be able to get in and out before the local crowd gathers. The waters running around fifty seven degrees this time of year, make sure you have your skins with you. I'll give you an hour to show me what you've got. I'm not committing or agreeing to anything. I'm merely going to watch you surf. THAT'S IT! DON'T GET ANY WILD IDEAS!

Sincerely,

R. Eden

Don't get your hopes up kid. I'm a has been. Unimportant history in the books. You're looking for something that just isn't there anymore. I hate to do this, but it's the only way you'll understand what I'm saying to you.

Chapter Five

"Where the hell are you going, Austin?" Lori questioned her best friend as she watched her race around their apartment gathering miscellaneous items.

"Surfing, of course! Why?"

"It doesn't look like it to me. Besides, we never made plans to go out today. Did you hear something that I didn't?"

Austin laughed at her skeptical friend. "I'm meeting Rory Eden this morning."

"No way? Why didn't you tell me? Wait, you lying ass, she doesn't want anything to do with you. Remember I was there...twice. You're lucky she didn't have us arrested."

"Yeah yeah, it's fine if you don't believe me. I was going alone anyway."

"Good, I'll see you on the twelve o'clock news tonight in jail for stalking her, and by the way, don't bother calling me to bail your ass out either. I have to pay the rent this week."

"Joke all you want." Austin grabbed her surf board and tossed her backpack over her shoulder. "I'm not sure when I'll be home, we're meeting in Redondo. Wish me luck!"

~ ~ ~

Rory's Audi screeched to a halt in the first parking space of the empty lot. She pushed the button to put up the convertible top and climbed out, noticing a red SUV pulling into the lot with a surfboard on the roof rack.

Austin got out of the truck, walking over to Rory. She was dressed in black board shorts, with a white and black rash guard shirt and black flip flops. Rory was wearing tan colored cargo pants and a white hooded t-shirt with her company logo on the back in blue and flip flops as well.

"You're late," Rory said, taking in the sight of the beautiful young blond as she removed her board shorts, showing off the black string bikini bottoms that barely covered her ass, before she stepped into her wetsuit. *Damn...don't look, Rory. She's way too young. You're turning into Martie.*

"Rory, I'm very sorry. My roommate had the truck and I had to wait for her to come home."

"Well, let's get this over with." Rory walked down the stairs and onto the sand. Austin followed with her board under her left arm. They stopped a little ways away from the parking lot. The beach was completely empty, except for a few seagulls and two men surfing off in the distance. Rory watched the line-up of waves as Austin waxed her board.

"It looks like the first two lines of the set are mushy.

Try dropping on the third, it has the best lip," Rory said, giving a bit of advice before sitting down on a beach towel.

"Thanks." Austin watched the set and immediately picked up on Rory's observation. She grabbed her board and headed out into the waves.

~ ~ ~

Rory watched Austin drop on her first wave, noticed right away that Austin surfed goofy-foot, with her left foot in the back and her right foot leading, just as she had done.

Austin floated on top of the wave lip, performing a few tail-slides, carving through the water, before getting pitched off her board when she'd tried to do a top-turn. *Damn it, Austin, get over these nerves already. You're going to flop on your ass in front of her.* Austin chided herself as she concentrated on the set, choosing the third wave again. This time, she got her bearings, patting down the nerves and ripping the wave. She started with a three-sixty, followed by a few left and right carves, and then a tail-slide into a nose-grab aerial that landed backwards. Then, she spun around in a cut-back motion with a hand drag that went into a left carve and finally a stall as she pitched herself off the board. Rory sat on the beach amazed at the raw talent of the young woman. She undoubtedly had skill and style, but her technique and unique characteristics were what set her apart and those would most definitely need some cleaning up.

Austin looked like a drowned rat as she washed ashore with her board. Rory didn't budge from where she was sitting until Austin walked over to her, standing her board up in the sand.

"So, what did you think?"

"Well, Miss Tinsley..." Rory started.

"Please, call me Austin."

Rory's eye brows turned in as she almost lost her train of thought. "Okay fine, Austin, I do believe you have a very interesting form and it's definitely original. You're certainly talented, but even with the best there is still always room for improvement. You have a natural ability. That in itself is a great quality. You simply need to work on your technique and what makes you worthy of high judging scores. Basically, you have it—you just need to clean it up. You have old habits and those are the hardest to break."

Austin wasn't sure whether or not she should be happy or take that as being shot down. "So, Rory, what exactly are you saying?"

Rory smiled. "I'm sorry. I lost you with all the jargon. The business woman in me seems to lead my thoughts these days. It's been a while since I watched someone with raw talent like you have. You looked good out there, mate. I could definitely see you entering competitions and winning. You just need to work on a few things. With some major, as well as, minor adjustments, you'll come out with a very nice style. I don't think I have ever seen anyone ride as loosely as you do, yet still manage to control most of the wave. If you learn to master that, you'll be unstoppable," Rory said, smiling again.

Austin's face lit up with excitement. Hearing someone as well-known as the woman standing in front of her, say those words to her, meant everything. Rory was an admirable and remarkable woman in Austin's eyes. No matter how hard Austin tried to remember that this was a professional meeting, her heart skipped a few beats staring into the light blue eyes looking back at her. *Lori if you could be here right now you'd swear I was dreaming. Somebody pinch me!*

"So this means you'll do it, right?"

"Do what?" Rory looked confused.

"Train me of course. We had a deal."

"I-uh, well it's like this, Miss Tinsley…"

"Austin."

"Huh?"

"My name is Austin."

"Yes, uh…Austin, look I really don't have the time to devote to you. You really need some guidance and instruction. For one, I haven't been in the water in years and I just…" She let out a small sigh. "I just can't see myself being the one to do this for you. I'm sorry. I will do everything in my power to find you the best trainer."

The huge smile on Austin's face disappeared as quickly as it had arrived.

"I don't want anyone else. Rory, I sought you out purposely. I've told you before, I don't care about your company. This has nothing to do with me riding for Eden Boards. You're a very reputable woman in this industry. I admire and respect you greatly. I came to you because I believe you're the one that can help me. Don't give up so easily, please." *I have a connection to you that I know you feel too. Damn it, I know I'm not making this up.*

"Austin, I agreed to come here and watch you, and I did that. I even threw in my advice and opinions. You have to realize I don't surf anymore. I run my company now. Like I said, you're a talented young woman and I can see you going far with the correct guidance. I can do my best to help you with that, but only in the ways that I *can* help you."

The morning crowd began filling up the beach around them as both women headed up to the parking lot. Austin put her board away and slipped her tank top back on. Rory was glad she didn't have to fight herself to look elsewhere, instead of at the very nice-looking hard body in front of her that Austin had covered up.

"I'll email you as soon as I find out some information for you. I'll toss around a few names and see what I can come up with. Trust me, Austin, this *is* the best way that I can help you."

Rory walked around to the driver's side of her Audi and unlocked the door.

"Rory…"

"Yes?"

"Thank you for…uh…for this today. I really appreciate it."

"You're very welcome, Austin Tinsley. I look forward to reading about you when you do go pro and hopefully I'll see you sign with my company. Have a nice weekend." Rory got in her car and put the top down as she backed out of her parking space. The little blue sports car was gone before Austin could even start her SUV.

~ ~ ~

Austin walked into her apartment, setting her surfboard down in the corner next to Lori's as she looked around for her scrupulous roommate, who was nowhere to be seen. *Wonder where she went. Hmm...oh well, it's not like you're going to believe me anyway, Lori.* Just as Austin rounded the corner to the kitchen, Lori ran directly into her.

"Ouch!" Lori yelped as she crashed into her friend.

"Oh my God you scared me. What the hell are you doing?" Austin said, just as surprised to see her.

"I'm eating lunch. What the hell are you doing? I thought you went surfing?"

"I did. I left early to beat the locals. I looked around for you, but I figured you'd left when I didn't see you."

"I was in the kitchen the whole time. Want a sandwich?"

"Uh, no thanks."

"How was Redondo this morning? The surf report said it was up but you know their version of up."

"Actually, it wasn't too bad, north swell with about four, maybe five foot waves, past the break. The water was a little warmer than I expected. I had a few nice rides before the local rats took over. Rory wasn't too happy about me getting there late, but..."

"Excuse me. You honestly don't think I believe that she met you there, right?"

"Of course, I know you don't believe me, but I'm serious. Why would I make that up? Anyway, like I was saying, she gave me some advice and said I have a nice style. She also told me she'll set me up with someone who can train me. We argued about that and then she left."

"Why did you argue with her? Maybe you should listen to her, Austin. You know she hasn't surfed since in years. She sits at a desk all day. Why in the hell would she come out of retirement to train you?"

Austin felt her eyebrows furl together. "Damn it, Lori, we've discussed this a hundred times. I'm not in the mood to argue with you right now."

~ ~ ~

Rory ran upstairs to change into shorts and a t-shirt when she arrived home. *Come on, Rory, be truthful to yourself for once. You can't give into this girl. Not now, not ever. It's not fair to her, she doesn't understand and she probably never will. Let it go, she'll make it on her own.*

"What the bloody hell have you stepped in now, Rory? I think you're damn mind's gone walk about!" she sighed as she thought about her professional intentions versus the evasive actions she had taken during the past month with Austin. She sat on the couch in the den downstairs, staring at the flat screen TV. An hour later, she was asleep with a re-run of The Simpson's playing across from her.

~ ~ ~

Monday morning came up quicker than Rory had expected. She sat at her desk debating whether or not she should bother checking her inbox. Most of it was business as usual, except for the one from Austin, which of course she was reluctant to open. Martie stopped in her office quickly before they went into their meeting with the Snow Team. Rory minimized the mail window on the computer.

"Hey what's up?" Rory asked.

"Not much, when are you leaving for Aspen?"

"I'm not sure, ask Alex. She usually gives me my itinerary a few days before I travel. Why?"

"Just wondering. I'm planning on going to La Jolla that weekend, unless you have something you need me to do."

"No, I can't think of anything. Tell your mom I said hey. I wish I could go with you. I haven't seen her in over a year."

"I will. She asked if you were coming with me. She knows better though."

"Yeah, well my days of surfing until I passed out in the sand are over. We'd better go. I'd hate to be late for my own meeting."

~ ~ ~

Rory waited until Wednesday to read the email from Austin. She anticipated the worst, but hoped Austin would understand the reasoning behind her decision. She sighed as she sat back, putting her glasses on so she could read the screen. She still hated wearing them, but if the only repercussion she'd suffered from her traumatic accident were vision problems, then she was damn lucky.

To: R_Eden@EdenBoardsInc.com
From: ECSurfergrl@Media.net
Subject: Redondo

Rory,

I'd just like to thank you for the time you spent with

me at Redondo Beach this weekend. I really appreciate all of the advice that you gave me. Although, I'm not looking forward to learning from someone other than you, I can see where you're very busy. I'll do my best to try and learn some helpful tips from someone who is willing to take the time to train me. So, if you wouldn't mind passing my name off to a good trainer that won't cost me an arm and a leg, I'd be very thankful. Once again, thank you for all of your help and I look forward to being sponsored by your company in the future and possibly seeing you again soon.

Sincerely,

A.C. Tinsley

Rory was so shocked she had to read the paragraph twice. She took her glasses off, laying them on the desk. *What changed? I don't get it, Austin. One day you're begging me to train you and the next day you all of a sudden come to the realization that I don't have the time. This just doesn't make sense. What the hell?* Still stunned, Rory put her glasses back on and clicked on the reply button.

To: ECSurfergrl@Media.net
From: R_Eden@EdenBoardsInc.com
Subject: okay

Miss Tinsley,

First off, you're welcome. I'm glad I could be of

some help to you. As for a trainer, I'll have to go through a few lists to see who's available. I know you want to get started so I'll do what I can. I have to go to Aspen in two weeks, so I might not have someone for you until I get back. As I said before, I believe you are very talented and have one of the most unique styles that I've ever seen. I want to make sure you get the best training and advice. Don't worry about the money, I'll make sure it's something you can afford and if not, I'm sure I know someone who owes me a personal favor or two. I do have one question though, just out of curiosity, what made you change your mind so drastically?

Sincerely,

R. Eden

After she clicked send, she shut down her computer and rubbed the left side of her head, feeling the four inch scar above the throbbing ache as she pressed the intercom button.

"Alex?"

"Yes, Rory."

"I don't have any meetings for the rest of the afternoon, am I correct?"

"Yes Ma'am."

"Good. Hold all of my calls and reroute anything important to Martie's office."

"Yes Ma'am. Are you feeling okay, Rory?"

Rory laughed slightly. "Yes, Alex, I'm fine. I just have a few things I need to take care of this afternoon so I won't be returning to the office."

"Sure thing. Have a nice afternoon."

"You too."

Rory dialed Martie's extension and picked up the receiver when she answered.

"Hey, it's Rory."

"What's up?"

"I have a few things I need to do this afternoon, so I'm taking off."

"What! You have never left this building before dark. Are you feeling okay?"

"You sound like Alex. Yes, I'm fine. I just need to get out of here today. It's really nothing, I swear to you."

"I don't know. You're acting funny, Rory."

"Martie, you know me better than anyone. Therefore you should be happy when I'm stressed out and decide take some time for myself. Plus, I have some errands to run. I routed all of my important calls to you. I'll see you in the morning."

"Alright, call me later if you want."

"Okay, have a good afternoon."

"Yeah, you too." Martie hung up the phone knowing damn good and well something was up with her best friend, but getting Rory to talk about anything was like trying to pull teeth from a grizzly bear.

~ ~ ~

Rory ran into Carl, the security guard, as she entered her office building the next day. She felt refreshed after using the extra time off the day before to rest and relax. She'd taken half of a pain pill to stop the agonizing headache and had swum a few laps in her pool to ease the

74

tension in her shoulders. She'd fallen asleep early, and awoke just before her alarm the next morning.

"Hello, Carl."

"Happy Friday the thirteenth, Rory."

Rory's eyebrows cringed together as she walked away. She'd heard the same line reiterated from the receptionist in the lobby as she came through the front door. *What the hell is with these people? It's just another bloody day. Get over it!* Rory stepped into the elevator and the doors opened on her floor with Alex standing in front of them.

"If you say something about the date today, I'm going to fire you," Rory said, squeezing past her and walking briskly down the hall.

Once inside of her office, Rory shut the door and let out a long breath. *Don't check it, today of all days. Come on you don't have the best of luck as it is. You finally get her to realize you don't have the time or the desire to train her, but now you can't seem to hand her over to anyone else. Bloody hell, Eden, you can't have your cake and eat it too! Everyone is already on tour. So, either you train the girl or give her to some crony who couldn't give two shits about her or her career. No matter what, you still have to check your email...shit.* She wasn't sure why she was so drawn to Austin or cared so much about her career. Hell, if it had been anyone else, she never would've replied to the first email and probably would have had the person arrested for stalking her by now, but the enigmatic young woman had weaseled her way into Rory's mind and now she couldn't get her out if it. She was astounded by the fact that she actually looked forward to the emails from Austin. "What the hell am I doing?" she said to the empty office as the intercom on her desk buzzed.

"What?" Rory asked.

"Really? That's you how you answer your intercom?" Martie teased.

"What the hell do you want?" Rory growled.

Martie laughed.

"Cut the shit, Cruz!"

"Yikes! Grouch! Happy Friday the thir—"

"Don't you dare say it! I swear I'll go through this phone."

"Who pissed in your corn flakes this morning?"

"No one. I'm just sick of hearing that fucking phrase. Got it?"

"Yeah."

"Good, now what is that you want?"

"I had forgotten to tell you that Leann Strong left this past Wednesday for Australia. She's going to be there for the Roxy Pro Saturday and Sunday and she's flying back Monday. I scheduled a post meeting with her for Wednesday at nine."

"Sounds good."

"That's all I needed." she paused. "Hey, Rory, get your head out of the sand. You've been acting really strange this week. I'm around if you need to talk without snapping someone's head off."

"Martie, I'm fine. I just have a lot going on. I find the Friday the thirteenth crap ridiculous and it irritated me with everyone saying it this morning."

Rory spun around in her chair, looking through the floor to ceiling window and down at the busy streets of Los Angeles. *Just check it, Rory. You know it's going to drive you nuts if you don't.* She couldn't take the suspense any longer, so she opened the email from Austin.

To: R_Eden@EdenBoardsInc.com
From: ECSurfergrl@Media.net
Subject: thank you

Rory,

Once again, thank you kindly for everything you have done for me. I know that you're very busy, and I'm grateful that you're taking the time out of your busy schedule to find me not only the best trainer, but also a personal friend of yours. I appreciate it more than you know. As for your curiosity, I have never given up on you training me, and I never will. But, for me to get anywhere in this sport, I have to start somewhere. Unfortunately for both us, you're too busy with your company, so I have to go with option number two. Rory, if I had my choice, it is, as it always will be, you. I've told you before. I'm not just a fan. You're my inspiration and I admire you. Your connection with the waves is something so rare that it will probably never be seen again. I only hope to feel a tiny part of that connection in my own surfing. It made you one of the greatest surfers in history.

I hope you enjoy your trip to Aspen. I'll be looking forward to hearing from you when you return. Please email me or call me at 454-8001 when you have found me a trainer. Again, thank you for everything.

Sincerely,

A.C. Tinsley

Rory read the email and pushed her chair out from under the desk. "Damn it, Eden, why the hell is this bothering you so much? You don't want to train her, yet you don't want anyone else to either." *You had better think fast because you're running out of excuses.*

~ ~ ~

The plane touched down on snow covered ground and taxied to its designated terminal. Rory was one of the first passengers off the jet. She headed straight for the baggage claim area, pulling her coat a little tighter around her. She hadn't been to the snow in years and the near zero temperature outside the airport made it balmy inside. Fifteen minutes later, her bag finally came around to where she was standing. Rory grabbed the black suitcase and headed for the car rental area at the front of the terminal. She was quickly escorted out of the line by one of the airport staff.

"Can I help you?" she asked.

"Are you Rory Eden?"

"Yes. Why?"

"You're car is waiting right out front for you," the man said, point out the window.

"Thank you."

Rory turned around and wheeled her suitcase towards the automatic doors. She saw the large black Cadillac Escalade SUV parked alongside the curb. She walked towards the vehicle and a tall, very well-built, handsome young man, with tan skin and jet black hair stepped in front of her. He was wearing a black suit with a black necktie and didn't look anywhere near as cold as she was.

"Rory?"

"Yes."

"My name's Byron. I'll be your driver as well as your security during your stay in Aspen. It's nice to meet you." The Hollywood-looking guy offered his hand and Rory shook it briefly. She was still in shock and trying to figure out exactly what he meant by security. She was freezing and at that point she wouldn't have cared if he was a serial killer. She got into the warm vehicle, pointing the heater vents directly at her.

"We should be going. I know you're very busy. The hotel concierge has given me your week long schedule," he said as he slid into the driver's seat.

Rory sat back as the car drove off toward the hotel. Security or not, she was glad she had a driver for the next few days. She'd never driven on snow and wasn't about to start now. *Security? What the hell is that supposed to mean? I don't need a personal body guard… Alex. You're trying to make me fire you, aren't you?"*

She finally settled into her suite and ordered up room service, instead of going down to the hotel restaurant. She'd found out from the hotel manager that Byron was on call twenty-four hours a day and readily available if and when she needed to leave the hotel. She was about to sit down and eat the succulent meal in front of her, when the phone rang.

"Hello?"

"Hey it's me. How's Aspen? See any hotties yet?"

"Martie, I should've known you set this up."

"What are you talking about?"

Rory sat on the couch, putting her feet up on the coffee table with her grilled chicken salad sitting in her lap. "My male hottie bodyguard, does that ring a bell?"

"Um no, but that's interesting though. Too bad you're a lesbian," Martie laughed.

"Cut the shit and tell me exactly why I have personal security while I'm here," Rory said between bites. "And no one knows I'm a lesbian except for you."

"That closet must get awful lonely," Martie teased. "I didn't make your arrangements, so I have no idea. Maybe Alex didn't want you to be bombarded with media, fans, or whoever else wants to bother you."

"I know what you're saying, but this is a little much. I don't need security. I'm a washed up retired surfer."

"Rory, you're a multi-millionaire and you have people falling at your feet wanting you to sponsor them. It makes sense."

Rory sighed. "He's my driver, so I guess I can pass him off as that."

"Yeah, so anyway tell me what it looks like. Is there snow?"

"Of course there's snow, dipshit. It's a winter wonderland and I'm at a snowboarding event at the top of a mountain, hello! I'm freezing my bloody ass off. It's barely two degrees outside. Oh hey, remind me to thank Alex for putting me up at this beautiful hotel. I have a fully stocked mini-bar and a gorgeous snow covered mountain view from my balcony."

"Sounds great! Now you just need a naked snow bunny to heat up your room."

"Martie, is sex the only thing you ever think about?" Rory chided.

"No, not the *only* thing."

"Smartass. Anyway, I'm planning on seeing our riders tomorrow."

"Yeah, I know. Stephen said he set everything up so you can meet all of them tomorrow morning. I emailed all of that to you."

"Thanks. I haven't checked me inbox yet. I'm hoping to sneak in a chat with a few other people while I'm here. Mainly, Adler Troy. I really don't want to fork out the money to buy her out of her contract, but she's the damn face of women's snowboarding. She could be the greatest investment I ever make."

"I definitely agree with you. She's at the top of her game and she's easy on the eyes too. Wait until you see her."

Rory huffed. "She's married, Martie. Keep your mind on business and out of the gutter."

"No she's not. I think I read somewhere that she got divorced recently."

"Either way, I'm not here to sleep with her. I just want her using our equipment and I want her name affiliated with my company."

Rory finally got off the phone and set up her laptop on the desk. She read the information from Martie, remembering that she had already received an email from Austin and had not responded to it. *Oh get over it, Rory. She's stuck on your past. There's nothing you can do to change it. Find her a trainer and move on.* "Well, I guess I could actually call her. Like that's going to help. Find someone for her and be done with it."

~ ~ ~

Rory met with her riders first thing Saturday morning then spent the rest of the day watching the practice runs and prelims. She'd also had a few interviews and photo ops for several snowboard magazines as well as ESPN shots. At the end of the day, Byron drove her back to the hotel. Rory stood outside on her balcony staring out at the snow covered mountain. The way the moon shone down on the snow was breathtaking. Amidst a beautiful white covered backdrop, the only thing on Rory's mind was Austin and the gut wrenching idea of someone else training her.

The next day, Rory was on the mountain early to watch the qualifying for the Superpipe. A few of the riders who had contacted her company about sponsorships were standing nearby, awaiting their turn on the pipe. Rory had watched them all the day before, but she zeroed in on the only rider in her sights, watching as Adler Troy made her way over to the group with her long, curly blond hair flowing under her ski cap. She was beautiful, Rory couldn't deny that, but Adler Troy was a whole lot more than good looks. She was a fierce competitor, a star in her sport and a headstrong woman with a fire in her eyes that reminded Rory of herself many years ago.

"Excuse me, Adler? May I speak with you a minute?" Rory asked.

"Sure," Adler said, walking over to her.

"I'm Rory Eden, with Eden Boards," Rory stuck her hand out.

"Yes. Hi, I thought that was you. I saw you yesterday, I think."

"I was here, yes. I was hoping you and I could sit

82

down and talk sometime before this weekend ends," Rory said.

"I'd love to. How about tonight?"

"That sounds great. I'm staying at the Premier Aspen Hotel. Would you like to meet there? I know there are a lot of spectators around town. I'm in a private suite."

"That's probably better than trying to go somewhere local." Adler smiled. "I can be there at six."

"Great, I'll have Byron escort you in when you get there," Rory said, nodding towards the man standing a few feet away.

"See you this evening then," Adler replied, walking back over to get in line for qualifying.

Rory went back to the bottom of the pipe to join the other spectators as each rider made three attempts at a clean pass down the pipe. She watched as Adler dropped in, carving across the bottom of the pipe to the other side into a back-nine, spinning nine hundred degrees, before landing and carving back across to the opposite wall. She maintained her height, staying at least ten feet out of the pipe as she did trick after hair-raising trick, all the way to the bottom. Rory cheered with the rest of the crowd. Adler Troy had qualified first with that run, to no one's surprise. She was on top of the world and at the top of her game.

Chapter Six

Rory spent the rest of the day talking with other sponsors and watching a few different events that she had riders participating in. She also made her way over to the snowmobile track to watch the daredevil guys doing crazy tricks and flipping four-hundred pound snowmobiles off the end of huge ramps. The adrenaline rush she got from just watching them was incredible. She could only imagine what the riders actually went through while performing some of those tricks.

True to her word, Adler arrived at six and Byron took her through the service entrance of the hotel and used the service elevator to sneak her up without the people in the lobby seeing her. Rory had already called ahead for a bottle of wine to be brought up which had arrived at her door at the same time as Adler.

"Come in," Rory said, waving her in as the waiter set the wine on the coffee table, opening the bottle and pouring both glasses. "I'm glad you could join me."

"Me too. I used to watch you surf when I'd catch it

on TV and I've actually seen you surfing live a few times too," Adler replied, sitting down on the couch.

"Oh really?" Rory asked, taking a seat in the adjacent chair. "You do drink wine I hope."

"Oh, yes." Adler smiled, taking the offered glass. "So, yeah, I surf a little in the summer between traveling around chasing the snow. I always go to California for a few weeks. I have a little bungalow near Huntington Beach."

"Wow, yeah, I definitely surfed that area back in the day. So, are you any good at surfing?"

"Oh, no way. I can hold my own with the local cronies, but snowboarding is my passion."

"I can certainly see that, which is why I invited you here. I know Stephen Silver has spoken to you about what our company has to offer, so I won't go into all of that. You know as well as I do, that you're the face of women's snowboarding right now and my company is up and coming and fighting for the top manufacturer spot. I'm here to talk to you about what we need to do to join forces and make Adler Troy the new face of Eden Boards."

Adler smiled. "As I told Mr. Silver, I actually own a few Eden Boards and bindings that I've purchased personally. Don't get me wrong, my current board sponsor is great and so is my clothing sponsor and so on, but I do like the idea of having the entire package and being the best of the best and using the best equipment. Mr. Silver mentioned that your company is looking for a lot more than just a snowboard sponsorship, am I right?"

"Yes, we're looking at covering you one-hundred percent from your clothing to all of your equipment."

"This is exactly what I've been looking for, but I'm bound to multiple contracts," Adler said, sipping her wine.

"I'm well aware of those contracts," Rory sighed. "I've been in contact with all of those companies in regards to you and since you manage yourself, I'll tell you that they think I'm going to pay millions to get you out of those contracts."

"Oh my God, that's ridiculous."

"Yeah, you're telling me. I will keep working on it until something changes their minds I guess. On a good note, we still have a few weeks before the Olympics. So, hopefully we will figure out a way to have you on our boards and wearing our clothing line before then."

"Rory, I know your story and I really like the way your company operates. I try to live my life as green as I can, and I know your company does a lot of donating and things like that for the environment as well as for injured riders and their families. You're not in it for the money or the fame, otherwise you wouldn't be sitting here right now talking to me. You'd have some peon doing it. I respect that. I'd like nothing more than to be the face of the snowboarding side of Eden Boards. Who knows, maybe I'll figure out a way out of those contracts sooner rather than later."

Rory poured them both another glass. "Well, now that we have all of that out of the way, tell me about Adler Troy. What made you start snowboarding? I've never been on a snowboard, just so you know, but I'll deny it if you ever tell anyone. It probably doesn't look so good if the owner of the company can't snowboard," she laughed.

"Yeah," Adler laughed too. "I've been snowboarding

all of my life. How about I teach you to snowboard and you teach me some of those surfing moves of yours?"

Rory felt the smile fade from her face. She thought of Austin and who might be teaching her surfing moves. She took a long swallow of wine. "Oh, I stopped surfing a long time ago. I'm afraid I don't remember many of those moves anymore," she replied. "But, I'd be willing to ride a snowboard, at least once." she smiled.

~ ~ ~

The next day, Rory watched different final events on the mountain, saving the best for last. She arrived at the superpipe in time to see the start of the women's half pipe final. Each woman took their first run down the pipe. Adler played it somewhat cautiously, moving down to second place with another rider, Amy Hendricks, sitting in first place. The women only had two runs and it came down to the final two. Adler dropped one of the best runs of her life, doing trick after trick flawlessly, moving down the pipe, throwing her hands in the air as she finished. Amy prepared to come down the pipe for her run as the crowd cheered loudly for the hometown favorite. Adler quickly unhooked her bindings, dropping her board in the snow as she ran over to the spectator line, pushing her goggles and helmet back. Rory was on the other side of the large crowd, but she watched, along with everyone else, as Adler threw her arms around someone, kissing them like a lover, causing the crowd to cheer even louder.

The final rider came down the pipe setting up for a great run as well, until her board slid out from under her on a landing, causing her to fall on her last trick. Adler had won another X Games gold medal. She ran over to hug the other riders and wait for the podium to be set up as the ESPN reporter caught up to her.

"First, let me say that was an awesome run. You have another gold medal for your wall and a fifth gold here at X Games," the reporter said into the microphone on live TV and over the loudspeaker for the crowd to hear. "Now, we all want to know who you ran to for a not so quick kiss when you finished your winning run." She smiled.

Adler looked back towards the spectator line. "That's my girlfriend. I love her so damn much," she answered, smiling brightly. Seeing the shocking look on the reporters face, she continued, "I just came out, didn't I?" She grinned and laughed.

Rory's jaw hit the ground. That was definitely something she hadn't see coming. She watched as Adler received her medal and took photo after photo as she made her way through the crowd. She spotted Rory, waving her over.

"Rory Eden, this is my girlfriend, Dr. Cason Macauley."

"Cason, this is the woman I told you about, whom I met with yesterday."

"Oh, right. It's nice to meet you," Cason said, sticking her hand out.

"It's nice to meet you too," Rory replied. "So, it looks like you just stirred the hornet's nest," she said to Adler.

"Yeah, well, I told you I'd figure a way out of those contracts." She smiled. "Honestly, I've been through so much in the past year. I'm finally ready to live my life and be happy. I don't care what anyone has to say about that."

"That's great. You won't have any problems from me. You and I have a lot more in common than you think," Rory said, winking at her.

Adler raised an eyebrow. "I'm not sure I…" She looked at Rory, and then focused on the man standing a few feet away. "Isn't that your husband?"

Rory laughed. "God, no. He's sort of my security and driver all rolled into one, but very few people know about me and I'd like to keep it that way, at least for now anyway."

"Your secret is safe with me." Adler grinned.

"Good. Well, I'm sure you want to go celebrate your gold medal and everything else. Give me a call if and when it heats up, which I'm sure it will."

~ ~ ~

Cason watched Rory walk away. "I can't put my finger on it, but there's just something about her."

Adler laughed. "You better not be putting your finger on it," she teased. "I know what you mean. She's really down to earth and someone I could definitely see as a friend. I think it's because she's been in the game, you know what I mean? She was a pro surfer and had a horrible accident that just about killed her. I remember hearing about it all over the news. I guess you could say the person she is now it what was resurrected from the ashes when her career went down in flames. She told me she hasn't surfed since. That's sad. I couldn't imagine never having the drive to snowboard again. It would kill me."

"Maybe that's what it is. She's genuine and you rarely see that anymore, especially with business people. Most of them are money grubbing assholes, like your current sponsors for instance."

"Exactly," Adler said, wrapping her arms around Cason's neck. "Let's sneak away before those assholes find me. I'll deal with them tomorrow. Right now, I want to be naked with you by the fire."

"If that's how you want to celebrate tonight, then I have absolutely no problem with it whatsoever," Cason replied, kissing her softly.

~ ~ ~

Rory spent the next two hours, posing with her riders for a few more magazine photos, and taking them to dinner to celebrate. Afterwards, she met up with a few people she knew from On The Edge magazine for a drink at Club Chelsea. When she'd been asked what she thought of Adler Troy coming out, she simply shrugged and said it didn't bother her. She'd overheard one of Adler's sponsors, who'd had a little too much to drink, talking about Adler. She stepped a little closer in time to hear him say that she was done in the snowboarding world because no one wanted a dyke representing their company. Rory left the club with a smile on her face.

Martie had called Rory's cell phone while she was at the club and left her a voicemail, so she'd returned the call when she got back to the hotel.

"Hey, Martie Mouse, I just got your message?"

"It's two thirty in the morning, Rory. Where the hell

are you?"

Rory laughed, knowing her best friend was probably just getting home as well.

"I went out for drinks with a few of the other sponsors and ran into some people from On The Edge. I had to celebrate. Did you watch the snowboard superpipe finals?"

"No. I just got home."

Rory laughed. "Oh my God, Martie. You missed Adler Troy coming out of the closet in front of everyone in the crowd and on live TV, after she won the gold medal of course. Wow, that girl can ride a snowboard!"

"No fucking way!"

"I'm serious. I even met her girlfriend. She's some kind of doctor."

"Holy shit! Damn, I wish I'd been there to see that!"

"Yeah, it was pretty crazy. The good thing is, her sponsors aren't so thrilled, so it looks like we'll be able to sign her as soon as they cut ties with her."

"Oh, man, that's great for us."

"Yeah, she's actually pretty cool. I spent some time with her yesterday. You'd like her."

"I knew she was lesbian."

"No you didn't. You just thought she was hot." Rory laughed.

"All women are lesbians deep down," Martie teased.

"Uh-huh. Keep telling yourself that."

"So, how did our riders do?"

"I was actually very impressed with our riders. Dalton Murphy and Stacey Holbritton both won gold in Slope Style. Our newest rider Ezekiel Jones came out with a silver in Snowboard X and bronze in Snowboard

Superpipe."

"Wow, I bet that was exciting as hell to watch."

"Yeah it was cool. Those girls can definitely carve! And the guys are fun to watch. Their tricks are unbelievable." *It's nothing like ripping on a perfect line-up of eight foot waves, but I guess it'll do!* "The bad part is, I'm still freezing my ass off and I have to be up early so I can go to the airport and change my flight coming home."

"You're coming back early?"

"Yes, all of the snowboarding events are over. The next two days are all skiing events and I don't really need to stay for those."

"Great, don't forget to call Alex in the morning and let her know that you changed everything. I guess I'll see you either tomorrow or Wednesday. Have a safe flight home."

"Thanks, bye."

~ ~ ~

Rory had been home for a few days, when she'd finally decided to stop fighting with the angel and devil on her shoulders. "Shit, Rory, just do it already!" she said, reaching for the phone just before it began to ring. *Talk about ironic.* She almost didn't pick it up.

"Hello?"

"G'Day to you too, my little ankle biter!"

Rory almost fell over backwards when she heard the voice with the thick Australian accent on the other end.

"Hey, Uncle Mick!"

"How the bloody hell are you, kid?"

"I'm good, how about you?"

"Not bad, zonked a bit. I just wrapped a Mickey Mouse case. Your mum's been busy as a cat buryin' shit too!"

"It sounds like the firm's doing well at least. I've been pretty busy myself. I just flew back from the Winter X Games. My riders came out on top though, so I had a good time."

"Good on ya."

"Thanks."

"You don't sound too stoked about it, kid."

"It's all good, Uncle Mick."

"Pig's ass, Rory! What's got your feathers ruffled?"

Rory knew her uncle could pick up on everything. Even three thousand miles away, he could tell something was bothering her. She walked over to the couch and sat down.

"Uncle Mick, it's complicated."

"What's wrong? I thought your company was doing great."

"It is. I couldn't be more pleased with my job."

"Alright, if you want me to help you, Rory, you have to spit it out. Is something wrong with Martie? Do you have a new mate?"

"It has nothing to do with Martie, and no I don't have a new mate, bloody hell," Rory sighed, hearing laughter on the other end of the line."It's not funny damn it!"

"Rory, I haven't heard you like this in a long time."

"I guess if anyone can give me some advice, you're the one to do it Uncle Mick and if you tell Mum, I'll be mad as a cut snake!"

"No worries."

"I had someone contact me, sort of a fan I guess you

93

could say. Anyway, she's a surfer and she wants me to train her to go pro."

"Well what did you say to the girl? Is she a shark biscuit?"

"Of course I said no, many times I might add. She kept on and on, so I finally went and watched her rip one about two weeks ago, and Uncle Mick she has talent…but, I just can't do that again. You know I haven't picked up a board in over four years. How in the hell am I supposed to teach and train someone to polish their skills?"

"It sounds a bit more complicated than that."

"It is. She's a huge fan of mine from way back and she doesn't quite understand that I don't surf anymore. I don't want to disappoint her. I'm a washed up has been," she sighed. "I told her I'd personally find her a trainer."

"You shouldn't sell yourself so short, kid. You're a lot more than a has been, especially if someone is seeking you out to train them. I understand if you don't want to do it. What I don't get is why you're letting this bust your gut."

"Because…shit, I don't want anyone else to train her, but I just don't think I can do it, Uncle Mick."

"Oh pig's ass! You can do anything you set your mind to, Rory. You know this. It sounds to me like you're having mixed feelings and not just about training her. Well, tell me, is she a beaut?"

"Of course she is, but she's a kid!"

"Give me some slack on the chain you're pulling. So, she's younger than you. What the bloody hell does that have to do with you being friends with the girl and helping her? Give it a whirl, Rory, and if it doesn't work out, then at least you tried and you can stop walloping yourself and walk away."

"I guess you're right. Martie's going to be pissed — she's been knocking this girl for a while."

"She's your best mate, Rory. Of course she's going to protect you. You just have to be fair with her. I'm sure it'll work out." *It might do you some good to get back on the other side of the sport again.* "So when are you coming back Down Under? Don't make me go walkabout across the pond to find your ass!"

Rory laughed with her uncle for a few minutes. "I'll be there in a month or so."

"I'll see you soon. I'll say hey to your Mum for you."

"Yeah thanks, see you soon."

"Hooroo," he said as he hung up.

Rory set the phone down and stared at the wall for a few minutes. *Damn you, Uncle Mick, why are you always right? Rory, it's not going to hurt you to be friends with her. Besides, she does need the proper guidance.*

Chapter Seven

As soon as Rory stepped out of the elevator, she stopped at Alex's desk.

"Hey, I need you to set up a meeting for me and Martie with the snow team for tomorrow afternoon."

"Sure thing."

Rory walked into her office and sat down behind her desk. *Now is as good a time as any.* She took her glasses off, tossing them on the desk. She rubbed her temples slowly, trying to ease the building tension and arrange her thoughts before she reached for the phone. She quickly dialed the number from memory.

"Hi, can I speak to Austin Tinsley please?"

"This is her."

"Uh, hey, this is Rory Eden. How are you?" Rory scolded herself mentally for her nervousness.

"Hi, uh...I'm good. How was your trip?" Austin nearly dropped the phone. She hadn't expected Rory to call her.

Rory smiled, thinking back to the events of the trip.

"Cold, but I had a great time."

"That's good."

"I haven't had a chance to find you anyone, yet. I have so many things going on right now."

"I totally understand how busy you are."

"Actually, the reason I'm calling is because I wanted to see if you were doing anything Saturday morning."

Austin's gray eyes bugged out of her head. *Did she just ask me out? No way!* "Uh, I'm not doing anything. I was going to go surfing but…"

"Great, I wanted to see you surf again. It might help me a little more with matching you up to someone."

"Sure, where do you want to meet?"

"Hmm, that's a good question. I haven't even seen the surf reports for this weekend. I just got back into town a few days ago and I've been in my office most of the time."

"I think Lunada is supposed to be happening this weekend. My friend Lori was talking about going up there."

"Sounds good. Call me on my cell sometime tomorrow and let me know the tides and the surf report. It's pretty rough out there and medium tide is the safest, so I'll meet you when it breaks."

"Great, I'll call you tomorrow and I'll see you Saturday morning."

Rory hung up the phone, nervously fidgeting with the pen in her hand. *There's no reason to be scared, Eden. You're just watching her surf. You're not getting in the water and she doesn't bite. Training her and sleeping with her are two completely different things. Calm down!* Rory tried to rationalize with herself, but it wasn't

97

working.

At the same time, Austin was sitting on her living room couch in shock. Lori walked through the front door of the apartment, stopping when she noticed the astonished look on her best friend's face.

"Who died?"

"Huh?"

"You look like you just saw a ghost or something, are you okay?"

Austin shook her head lightly. "Rory Eden just called me. She wants to meet Saturday morning to watch me surf again. She said she's trying to match me to a trainer who will work the best for my skills or something like that."

"Wow, that's cool. I hope you're not in over your head though, Austin. She's very restrained when it comes to her personal life. Don't get too close to her, you might get hurt."

"I know. Hey, she gave me her cell number and told me to call her tomorrow with the surf report at Lunada. She wants to go at medium tide so I have to tell her what time to meet me."

"Did you want me to go with you?"

"Nah, it might be better if I'm alone with her since she's so skittish about the whole situation."

~ ~ ~

Rory sat at the head of the table in the conference room with Martie on her left side. The snow team took up the remaining seats.

"As you all know, there was a lot of excitement in Aspen. Our riders performed well and Adler Troy shocked the world by coming out as a lesbian. I had a meeting with Adler before the Superpipe finals, expressing our interest in signing her. She was very interested and well, one thing led to another and she made a life-altering decision. She's gutsy, headstrong, independent, courageous, and driven to succeed. These are all qualities that I look for when signing sponsorship deals. Every snowboarder and surfer with factory equipment from Eden Boards is essentially a face for the company." She paused.

"With that being said, I want everyone to know that by the end of the day today, Adler Troy will be the newest face of Eden Boards. I spoke with her attorney this morning and she's being released from her contracts effective immediately. I'm excited to bring her on and I want to show the nation that Eden Boards doesn't see color, nationality, sexuality, gender, or anything else discriminatory. Adler's a great person, once you get to know her, which I'm sure you all will because I've invited her and her girlfriend to come and tour our facility at the end of the week. Stephen, I want to thank you for all of the hard work you did researching her contract information and working with the legal team to have her contract drawn up with us so quickly. We'll need to get her up and running and comfortable with our equipment as soon as possible. The Olympics are less than a week away. Let's meet in the morning to go over everything in more detail, Stephen."

He nodded.

"Martie is there anything you need to add?" Rory asked.

"Uh…" Martie looked at her notes. "I don't believe

so." She was shocked and a little pissed that she didn't know about Adler Troy's contract going into the meeting.

Everyone exited the room and Martie followed Rory into the elevator.

"Hey, what's going on with you? You confused me back there. Since when do we sign contracts that I know nothing about?"

"It's not a big deal, Martie. It literally happened all while I was driving to work this morning." Rory leaned back against the wall as the elevator started its ascent to their floor. When the doors opened she gestured for Martie to follow her with a quick nod of her head. Once inside her office, Rory shut the door and walked over to her desk, tossing the folder next to her computer monitor. She sat down lazily, removing her glasses and rubbing her face with both hands.

"You look stressed, Rory. Talk to me. I hate to see you like this. You've been acting funny for a few weeks now."

"I talked to Uncle Mick yesterday."

"Oh really, how's he doing?"

"Not bad. He's working like a mule. The firm's been pretty busy."

"How's your mom?"

"Busy running everyone's life in Queensland."

"Yeah well you know how your mom is, Rory. You're just like her when it comes to working and you know it. You would both rather bust your ass a hundred hours a week than have someone do it for you. It's a drive and ambition that I've never seen in anyone, except the two of you."

"Hmm…so anyway, he's looking forward to my going back there. I have a feeling they'll rig the plane so that I can't fly back to the states," she laughed and Martie snickered.

"Actually, Martie, I brought you in here to tell you something. I can't really discuss it right now, but I need you to know that I've made a decision that affects the company and…"

Martie jumped out of her seat. "What are you talking about, Rory? Are you selling the company? Taking on a partner? What the hell is it?"

"Calm down, it's nothing like that at all. In time, I'll tell you and everyone else. Right now, I haven't even made anything official. I finally made my decision yesterday after talking to Uncle Mick."

"Oh man, this can't be good. Are you in trouble or something?"

"No, of course not."

"Okay, then why the hell would a criminal defense lawyer help you make a decision about this company?"

Rory grinned. "It wasn't necessarily about the company. It's actually more personal than anything. He basically talked me through it."

Martie sat back down with one eyebrow raised up. *Personal? What the hell are you trying to say, Rory? Spit it out already.* She wasn't sure what to say or how to react to what Rory was telling her, so Martie just did the only thing she knew how to do when it came to her best friend.

"I trust you, Rory. Whatever it is, I'm sure it's fine and I hope it makes you happy. I've never known you to make a mistake or do something to jeopardize yourself or your career. Although, I am very curious to find out just exactly what it is that you're not telling me. I'm sure it'll come in due time." *I could probably beat it out of you, but then you'd hate me for a while. I hope you haven't gone and gotten yourself in too deep. Sometimes it's hard to swim when the water is over your head. I'm damn sure going to find out what's going on, whether you tell me or not. I'm not going to let you get hurt. You're up to something and I really don't like the smell of it.*

"Well, I guess that's it, then."

"So, what's next on the agenda with Adler Troy?"

"She's supposed to fax the signed contract back later today, then Stephen will schedule a session with her to get her measurements and all of the other stuff that we need for a new team member. I'm really excited about the future of our company, especially where snowboarding is concerned. I think you will really like her. She's a lot like us. I had a really good time, just hanging out and talking with her."

"Don't get me wrong, I think it's great that she's living her life out and proud. I just hope it doesn't negatively affect us."

"I don't think it will, honestly. I'm glad she did what she did. I think it expands the sport even further. Now, if we could just have a surfer come out, that would be icing on the cake." Rory smiled.

"You know, you could've been the one to do it," Martie said.

"Yeah well, so could you. I never told you to stop surfing the tour."

"I make a hell of a lot more money sitting in an office." Martie smiled. She'd left the tour to be at Rory's side and eventually help nurse her back to health. She'd never been as good a surfer as Rory, but she'd enjoyed being on tour and traveling the world, nonetheless. It had been fun with Rory beside her, but after Rory retired, she'd known it would never be the same, so she'd retired too. She still surfed for fun when she had the chance though.

~ ~ ~

Austin was sitting in her room, reading a magazine when Lori knocked on her door.

"I saw your light on. You're up early. The sun's barely shining," Lori said.

"I guess it was the excitement, who knows." Austin shrugged.

"Yeah, I just checked the surf report and it looks like it could be overhead swells by medium tide. I'll probably ride out there myself."

"Damn, I couldn't ask for a better day then. This is probably my last chance to prove myself to her. I feel like I've been called back for a second audition." Austin laughed.

"It sort of is, if you think about it," Lori said seriously.

"Okay, I was joking, but go ahead, Lori, make me more nervous than I already am."

"Why get so bent out of shape about *her,* Austin? I've seen you ride some of the sickest waves with a badass attitude and more confidence than anyone around. I've never known you to hesitate, Tinsley. Don't let her bother you. She obviously likes what she sees; otherwise, she wouldn't want to see it again. I doubt she'd be trying to help you out either."

"I know, I know. Last time she watched me, I fucking choked on the line, man. Luckily, I was able to talk some sense into myself and I came out okay, but what if it happens again? She's going to think I'm a loser or worse, scared!"

Lori sat back on the couch laughing hysterically.

"Damn it, Lori, this isn't funny!"

"Okay, calm down. You're definitely not scared. You have talent and she sees it. I don't care much for her these days with the corporate attitude, but she was a hell of a surfer and she knows her shit, Austin. The best thing for you to do is go early, take a run down the beach and clear your head. If you can't bring it together long enough to rip in front of her, how the hell are you ever going to surf a competition?"

"You're right, as usual. I just don't know if that'll work or not."

"Well, you'll never going to find out sitting here on your ass. Go on, get out of here. I'll be out there eventually. I won't go around you guys though. Just don't crowd the line, or I'll kick your ass, and then you'll definitely have something to be embarrassed about in front of her."

Austin laughed, shaking her head.

~ ~ ~

Austin was out in the water, floating on her board with her feet dangling over each side. She could barely see the shore, but her eyes were able to make out a certain blond-haired, blue-eyed woman, walking confidently through the dunes. As she swam in, Austin saw Rory looking at her through the waves. "Damn, you're cute. I'd do anything to kiss you again," Austin whispered, laughing at herself and shaking her head as

104

she walked out of the surf, to the woman waiting patiently for her.

"Morning," Rory exclaimed.

"Hey."

"I see you've beaten me to the punch this time."

"It's always good to get a head start. Besides, I made a terrible impression last time by showing up late, and then choking on the line. I figured what the hell, I'll go early and hope she's not there, so I can work out the bugs and get over my embarrassment."

Rory smiled. She was nervous deep down inside, for reasons she knew, but didn't want to admit. She hid it well on the surface.

"Well, shall we get the show on the road? The line's going off and looks like a pretty decent ride. It should work you a bit," Rory said, peering out at the waves.

"Yeah, I've been here for an hour. It's been tight all morning, hanging around five feet. It almost kicked my ass a few times."

"Great! I hope you're not completely worn out yet. This is the kind of wave that rides almost flat before it curls into a tight tube. It's the best for scoring major style points. Let me see what you can do."

"Sounds good." Austin grabbed her board and walked back towards the water as Rory sat down in the sand, with no clue as to what she was about to see.

All Rory knew was this girl intrigued her with a lot more than just her surfing style and that scared her. She'd never let anyone get close to her, except Martie, and Martie had been like a sister to her for nearly half her life. No, the feelings Austin stirred in her were much different.

Rory's nerves slowly settled as she watched Austin paddle out. She observed her waiting patiently for the perfect set. Austin began paddling like a mad woman, before popping up on her board and dropping on the face of a flawless five foot wave.

Austin's body molded into perfect form as her board ripped smoothly along the wave. Her right hand hung low, dragging softly through the water as it rushed under her. She quickly jerked her body, throwing the board into a tail slide, grabbing the right rail as she cut back, riding along the face of the wave, carving left and right, before spinning a three-sixty, launching into an aerial nose grab. She landed it almost perfectly, turning into a one-eighty spin, slashing across the top of the wave, throwing a spray of water in her wake.

Rory sat wide-eyed, amazed at what she had witnessed over the past half-hour as she'd watched Austin rip wave after wave with total insanity. Part of her wanted to jump up, screaming and shouting, because she was stoked at the limitless, free spirited way that Austin surfed, but the rational side of her wanted to call Austin in and explain to her the difference between control and chaos, mostly for the sake of the judges in a competition. *I've never seen anything like her. How the hell do you teach someone to control their best feature? Wild and untamed is her style. You can't take that away from her. What are you about to get yourself into, Eden? This is definitely going to be one hell of a challenge.* Rory looked back out towards the waves and was shocked to see Austin standing almost directly in front of her, toweling off her hair.

"Cat got your tongue?" Austin said, shaking her hair out.

"Uh…what…no I…" Rory stumbled for words as her blood raced south, abandoning her brain. "I was just thinking of something." Rory shook her head, trying to get her mind to refocus. She would be stupid if she lied and said she wasn't attracted to Austin. Anyone with a damn pulse would be attracted to her, but she needed to get her head on straight or she'd be in a world of trouble. She stood up, looking intently at a pair of gleaming gray eyes. "You looked good out there. Your style is so incredibly different from anything I've ever seen. You're extremely gifted, Austin."

"Thank you, Rory. That means a great deal coming from you."

"I know you're pretty beat since you've been out here for a while, but would you like to take a walk?" *Why do I feel like I have a bloody schoolgirl crush? This has to stop or I'm never going to be able to do this.*

Austin was taken off guard, but recovered quickly. "Uh, sure. Let me go put my board in my truck and get out of these skins."

Rory waited and Austin returned a few minutes later wearing warm-up pants and a long-sleeved t-shirt. Her wet hair had slowly begun to dry in the sun.

"Shall we?" Rory nodded.

Rory walked slowly and Austin fell in line next to her, reminding her of the night they walked along the beach on New Year's Eve. The memory of their brief kiss toyed with her mind. Their hands touched momentarily from the closeness, before both women inched away, avoiding further contact.

"So, you really think I'm good enough?"

"Of course, with a little guidance you'll be competing

in no time. You have a gift, Austin; a very unique gift."

"Wow, I don't know what to say to that. You amaze me. I can't believe you're basically telling me that you think I'm good enough to go pro." The smile on Austin's face was immense. It almost hurt to smile that hard and feel that happy inside. "Man, I could kiss you, Rory Eden."

Rory stopped walking. She stared at Austin, slack jawed. "Excuse me!"

"I said I could kiss you. Calm down, it's a figure of speech."

"Yes. Yes of course it is, I mean, you caught me off guard." Rory's stomach did a flip.

"The reason I asked you to take a walk with me is because I wanted to talk to you. I've been doing some thinking and well, I can't seem to match you with any trainers that owe me a favor. So, I've decided to uh…take it upon myself to train you."

Austin threw herself at Rory, wrapping her arms around Rory's neck. Rory felt warm tears running down Austin cheek as it pressed against her own. She hadn't expected a reaction quite like that. She stood stiffly for a second, before threading her arms around Austin's waist, holding the young woman as she wept with happiness.

As Austin pulled away, she wiped the moisture from her face, looking up into the most sincere baby blue eyes that she'd ever seen.

"I…uh…I don't know where to begin. Wow, thank you so much, Rory. You have no idea what this means to me. It's like a dream come true. I promise not to fail you or make a fool out of you," she rambled.

"I'm not worried about that, Austin. I believe you have talent and helping you with this is the right thing to do."

~ ~ ~

It was after five p.m. when Austin arrived back at her apartment. Lori was passed out on the couch with a rerun of King of the Hill playing on the TV. She walked by, slapping Lori's foot that was hanging off the couch, on the way to her room.

"Wake up, we have some cele-fuckin-brating to do!"

Lori rolled over, yawning and stretching. "What the hell, Austin."

Austin came back out of her room, half-dressed and on her way to the shower. "Wake up, we're going out!"

"Since when?"

"Since Rory Eden just offered to personally train me herself."

Lori jumped off the couch. "Get out! You're fucking with me, right?"

"Nope!"

"What the hell? How did you get her to do that, Houdini?"

"I have no idea. One minute I was surfing and the next she wanted to walk down the beach. Then out of the blue she said it. Trust me, I was shocked. I almost kissed her!"

"Thank God you didn't do that. You'd probably need a dentist instead of a trainer."

"No shit!"

"Wow! I have no idea what to say. You pulled it off. I can't believe it. One day you're sitting here telling me it's your dream to know her and be trained by her and here you are basically making it all come true. You have a huge set of balls, Austin Claire Tinsley! I couldn't be happier for you."

~ ~ ~

Twenty-four hours had gone by since Rory had stood on the sandy beach, basically making Austin's dreams come true. She still couldn't believe she'd actually done it. To top it all off, she was thinking of doing something even more extreme than she'd ever envisioned. She sat on the couch in her living room, dialing a number from memory.

"Hello?"

"Hey, this is Rory. How's it going?"

"Hey!"

"So, has it sunk in yet?"

Austin chuckled. "Yes, I guess you can say it finally has. I had to pinch myself this morning to make sure I hadn't been dreaming. You're not calling because you've changed your mind are you?"

"No." Rory laughed. "I'm actually calling because I need to meet with you either today or sometime tomorrow between my meetings; your choice. I need to get some information from you such as your weekly schedule."

"I see, well I'm free this afternoon. My roommate Lori and I surfed the break at Hermosa this morning."

"Nice. How was it?"

"Close to five, but it closed out at mid tide so we weren't out long."

"Ah, that sucks."

"Yeah, so you want to meet somewhere or should—"

110

"Where do you live? I don't think you've ever told me."

"We have an apartment off Termino Avenue. We pay out the ass for the little two bedroom place, but it's worth it since it's in a nice area and close to everything, including the beach."

"You're not too far from me then. For some reason, I figured you lived across town."

"Nope."

"I have some errands to run first, but we can definitely meet later today. I'd prefer that, since I have a hundred things going on this week at the office."

"Sure, I know you're a busy woman. I guess we need to work out some kind of payment plan or something too."

"We'll get to that. So anyway, it's what, one o'clock now? I should be done around five or six. Is that okay?"

"Sure, where are we meeting?"

"I'll be at Seal Beach. If you want to meet at the pier, we can have dinner at Ruby's."

"Sounds good, I'll see you around five-thirty."

~ ~ ~

Rory stood at the end of the pier, watching the small waves roll in and listening to them crash against the pilings. She turned to see Austin walking towards her, dressed in loose fitting low rise jeans and a long-sleeved t-shirt that barely touched the top of her jeans, letting the tanned skin on her stomach peak when she moved. Her thick, wavy hair was pulled up off her neck in a loose bun, showing off the tiny gold hoop in the top cartilage of her left ear. Rory's chest burned with an aching need to reach out and touch her.

"Hey you," Rory said, leaning her back against the rail, putting more distance between them as she crossed her legs at her ankles.

"Hey." Austin smiled, looking into the gorgeous, clear blue eyes staring back at her. "Did you get all of your errands done?"

"Yeah, finally," Rory replied.

Austin moved next to her and leaned against the rail, peering over the side.

"You going to jump?" Rory teased, turning around and placing her hands on the rail.

"Ha, of course not. I might be dare-devilish, but I'm not suicidal." Austin laughed."So you wanted to know my schedule."

"Well, it would be nice to know when we can train. I work such a hectic schedule, and right now, I'm in and out of town just about every week. I figured I could balance around your free time since I have none."

"Ah, I see. I know you're really busy, Rory. I don't expect you to be with me every free minute that you get. I understand you're a corporate monster."

"A what!"

"You've joined the masses of the business world. They're a different breed of people. I'm waiting to see you in a pantsuit and heels."

"Okay, that'll never happen. I guess I have changed though."

Austin broke out into fit of laughter. "You should see the look on your face. I'm sorry. I didn't mean it in a bad way. Honest."

"Yeah, yeah. Anyway, you want to go inside Ruby's

and grab something to eat? We can sit down and discuss this boisterous calendar of yours."

The women were seated in a small quiet booth next to one of the windows and placed their dinner order with the waitress who sat them.

"So?" Rory questioned.

"I'm a junior at Cal State, so I have classes during the week."

"That's awesome. I graduated from UC San Diego. What's your major?"

"Marine Biology. I work at the Aquarium full time and I get partial class credit for it, so I actually take my classes online. The only time I'm ever on campus anymore is for exams."

"Wow, I'm definitely impressed," Rory said, looking at the young woman across from her. She felt like she was seeing her for the first time. She was not only talented and cute as hell, she was smart and sophisticated. Rory felt the connection between them pull her a little bit deeper.

Austin smiled shyly. "Thanks."

"What's your degree in?"

"I double majored. BA in Design and BS in Engineering."

"Damn! That must've been hard."

"Yes it was, considering I moved back to the states after high school to go to college and surf the Pro Tour. I busted my ass. When I look at the degrees on the wall in my office, I don't remember how I ever got everything done, but somehow I pulled it off."

"Where did you go to high school?"

"Well, I lived in Santa Cruz until I was seven, then

we moved to the Gold Coast. I lived there until I graduated from high school. I moved to La Jolla right after that, and stayed there through college. I spent most of my time going back and forth between La Jolla and Hawaii while I was on the tour."

"Wow, I'd always thought you were Australian. I mean, I know you said you were born in California, but I was shocked when you'd told me that."

"Yeah, I guess everyone sort of thinks the same thing. So anyway, do you work Monday through Friday or—?"

"Well most of the time, I work Monday, Tuesday, and Wednesday in two six hour shifts each day at the aquarium. My online classes are Thursday and Friday. Then, I spend my weekends catching up on sleep or extra school work. I surf pretty much every morning unless it's flat or the weather is bad and sometimes I go in the afternoons or the weekends if it's breaking over four feet."

"Damn, I thought I had a rough week."

"I'm almost done with school, so it's not that bad. If things go my way, I should graduate in the spring."

"I thought you said you were a junior?"

"I am, but I took college classes in high school and I started college a year early, because I graduated high school a year in advance with a scholarship. I went to Coastal Carolina University back home and transferred out to Cal State after my first year. So, I'm actually halfway through my senior credits and will be able to graduate early, hopefully, but Cal State has me listed as a junior. Working at the aquarium has really helped me out a lot. Luckily, Lori was able to transfer too, so she moved here with me."

"Wow, you continue to impress me," Rory said.

Austin smiled shyly. "I hope that's a good thing."

Rory paid the bill after a semi-argument from Austin and they left the restaurant, walking along the pier. The sun had set, cooling the temperature slightly. Rory took a deep breath, leaning over the rail. She wasn't sure when she'd actually made the decision, but nonetheless here she was and she couldn't talk herself out of it. *Too late to back out now.*

"Austin, I uh…I know you're very busy with school and all, but…well I want to do everything I can to help you and I think getting to know you better is a good start. We need a good foundation if we're going to build a working relationship."

Austin had a questioning look in her gray eyes. "Okay…"

"I'm leaving on Thursday morning for Stockholm, Sweden. I'm going to the snow events of the winter Olympics and I'd like it if you'd join me. I think…"

"What!" Austin's jaw dropped. *Did she…no way! Oh my God, she just asked me to go to Sweden with her. I must be dreaming.*

"You don't have to go. I just thought I'd ask you since I'll be gone over a week. I figure I can kill two birds with one stone. I'll be working, but I'll also have some time to talk to you and get to know you better." *Way to crash and burn, Eden! I told you this wasn't going to work. Training her is a bad idea and becoming friends with her is totally out of the question.*

Austin was almost too shocked to say anything to the woman standing in front of her. Rory's soft blue eyes twinkled in the moonlight.

"Wow, I uh..." She cleared her throat. "I don't know what to say. I'd love to go with you. Are you sure that's okay?"

"Of course it is, on my end I mean. What about you with work and school and everything?"

"Well, as long as I have access to a computer I'm fine with my classes and we don't have any exams coming up anytime soon. I'm sure work won't be a problem. How often does a girl get to go to the Olympics?" she beamed.

"Not very often I guess, but you'll get to see the inside of things. It's going to be cold as hell and we'll be up to our assholes in snow."

"Sounds like fun!"

"Really?"

"Yeah, I think it would be good for us to sort of get to know each other. Besides, I haven't seen snow in years!"

"I'm glad you agree with me. I just didn't want to cross any ethical boundaries or anything like that. You have the fundamentals of surfing down, but I think if I can get to know you as a person and not just a surfer, then I can try my best to show you how to hone your skills. Surfing is as much mental as it is physical, and anyone that tells you otherwise, is full of shit."

Austin smiled. "Once again, you've amazed me. I agree completely."

"Good, I should probably get going. I'll call you tomorrow with all of the details and to make sure everything is okay with work and school. Austin, I don't want any of this to get in the way of your classes. If there is anything I can teach you, let it be the fact that education is the most important thing in your life. I will

116

not interfere with that. Do we have a deal?"

"Of course. What about payment. We didn't discuss that."

"Don't worry about paying me. I'm not doing this for the money. I'm doing it because I see something in you and I want to see you succeed."

"Okay."

Chapter Eight

Monday morning, Rory strutted out of the elevator, stopping at Alex's desk.

"Good Morning, Rory."

"I need to see you in my office to discuss my travel arrangements for Sweden. By the way, have you seen Martie yet?"

"No, I don't believe she's here. It's still a little early for her."

"Good, I'll speak with her later."

Rory continued walking to her office. She'd just sat down in her chair when Alex knocked on the door.

"Do you have my itinerary completed?" Rory asked.

"Yes, I finished it Friday," Alex replied, sitting in the chair across from her.

"I was hoping you'd say no. There are a few changes that I need you to make today."

"Okay." Alex stared with a blank look on her face. She was completely confused. Rory had never changed her travel plans at the last minute.

118

"I'm bringing a guest with me and she will be with me throughout the trip. So, please make sure she has an adjoining room. Also, make sure her name is on all of my official passes and guest invitations, since she will accompany me to the events and dinner parties." Rory paused. "I think that's all. If I'm forgetting anything please let me know."

"I believe you covered everything, except for her name."

"Oh." Rory laughed. "Austin Tinsley."

"Great, I have everything noted here and I'll make all of the changes effective immediately."

"Thank you and Alex…please make sure this stays between you and me. I don't need everyone on my back asking to go along with me on trips. Martie is enough to handle all by herself."

Alex smiled. "Yes ma'am."

~ ~ ~

Rory waited until after lunch to call Austin. Everything was still a go and Austin seemed genuinely excited about the trip. Her mind drifted to Martie. She knew she had waited long enough and now was as good a time as any to start the fight she knew would happen. She pressed the intercom button.

"Hey, you got a second?" Rory asked.

"Yeah, what's up?" Martie sat back in her desk chair.

"Come down to my office. I need to talk to you about something."

Martie clicked off the intercom and walked down the hall. Alex was busy typing away on her computer, paying her no attention as she passed by.

"Good Morning," Rory said cheerfully.

"Excuse me?" Martie raised an eyebrow, sitting in the same seat Alex had occupied.

Rory burst out in laughter.

"What the hell is going on, Rory? You've been acting really strange for the past week."

"Nothing really. I just thought I'd let you know that I'm not going to Sweden alone."

"Huh....why not? Who's going and what the hell for?"

"Calm down. It's no big deal. I've asked a friend to come along with me."

"Who is this 'friend'?"

"No one in particular. I just thought I'd tell you before someone else did."

"I don't understand, Rory. Who is it? This isn't like you to keep things from me."

"I'll tell you but you have to promise to calm down and let me explain."

"Fine..."

"It's Austin Tinsley."

"What!" Martie shouted loud enough for the entire floor to hear her. "Are you crazy, Rory? What the hell are you thinking taking her with you? Why the fuck are you even talking to her?"

"It's okay, Martie. I'm friends with her."

"How the hell did this happen? Oh my God, you slept with her!"

"What? No. It's nothing like that. I...well...I'm sort of training her."

"What did you just say?" Martie whispered.

"You heard me. I'm helping her out. The only reason I'm taking her with me is to get to know her better."

"You mean to tell me you're training her to surf? Isn't that what she kept coming around here for?"

"Yes, she finally got to me, I guess. Martie she's good...damn good. I've never seen a style so unique."

"You don't have the time or the heart, Rory. It kills you to even work around it anymore and now you mean to tell me you've gone and watched her surf?"

"Yes...but...."

"But nothing...what the hell has gotten into you? I thought you've been acting funny. What's really going on with her?"

"There's nothing 'going on'. She's a baby, that's more *your* style isn't it?"

"Very nice, don't try and turn this fucked up mess around on me, Rory Eden. I can't believe you've gotten yourself mixed up with that girl. She's trouble. We both knew that from the beginning."

"She's a nice girl, Martie, and she just needs someone to give her a chance. I'm that someone."

"So why in the hell do you have to take her to the fucking Olympics with you? I'm your best friend and the vice president of this company. If anyone else should be going, it should be me! I think I've earned that right!"

"Calm down, Martie. Look, before I even start training her I need to get to know her better. I figured with my hectic schedule around here this is the best way. She has nothing to do with this company. This is something personal that I decided to do on my own."

"I think you let your Uncle Mick talk you into this. What was his opinion?"

"He told me to do what I felt was right. I think training her is a good idea. Yes, it's going to be hard and

I've told her before that I'm a washed up old sock. I even offered to set her up with someone, but what I see in her, I don't think anyone else will see. I'm not asking for your permission, I'm asking you to understand…as a friend…my best friend."

"I can't back you up on this…I just can't. I think she's going after something and using her surfing skills to get to you. I don't trust her…not at all."

"Okay fine, if that's how you want to be about it, then there's nothing I can do to change your mind."

"Is that all?"

"Yes."

"Good." Martie stood up and walked out of the office, making sure to shut the door a lot harder than anticipated, causing a loud thud to echo through the hallway. *Damn you, Rory, you're in trouble and you don't even see it. I could kick this girl's ass. I swear I don't know how she did it, but she got to you.*

~ ~ ~

The car service that Rory had hired to take her and Austin to the airport arrived on time. She handed the driver her suitcase, and slid into the backseat with her briefcase, giving him Austin's address before he closed her door.

When they arrived at Austin's apartment, she was already outside, holding her suitcase. The driver helped her with her bag and held the door.

"I'm so excited I could barely sleep last night," Austin said, sliding in next to Rory.

"We have a long flight, so there will be plenty of time for that."

~ ~ ~

"Good afternoon, ladies. May I get you a soda, coffee, or a mixed drink?"

Rory looked over at Austin, who had her face glued to the plane window. "Do you want anything?" she asked.

"Uh...no, I'm fine thanks," Austin replied without looking away. She'd flown a few times since she'd moved to California, but this was the first time that her view wasn't obstructed by the wing of the aircraft.

"I'll take an ice water, please," Rory said.

The flight attendant smiled and walked away. Rory just shook her head at the young blond sitting next to her as she opened the novel that she'd brought with her.

The women had eaten dinner and then breakfast on the long sixteen hour, overnight flight to Stockholm. Luckily, they were in first class and had plenty of room to stretch out and sleep. When they arrived, the temperature was in the low teens and bitter and the ground was completely snow covered. They retrieved their bags at the baggage claim area after going through customs and Rory led Austin out of the airport, to a waiting Mercedes SUV. The driver loaded their baggage and then held the door for them.

"I believe you are heading to Dalarna, yes?"

"Yes, that is correct. We're staying at the Kläppen Resort," Rory replied.

Austin was surprised that the man spoke and understood English. The drive through town and up the mountain had been quick. Austin was amazed at the beautiful structure as the ski resort came into view.

"This ski park is where all of the snowboarding events will be taking place," Rory exclaimed.

"It's huge," Austin said, taking in the large building and surrounding mountain tops. Everything was covered in bright white snow and glistening in the sun.

The concierge made it a point to run out and introduce himself to the women and help with their luggage. Their rooms weren't much bigger than a full-sized hotel room with a kitchenette, a small living space and a king sized bed, but they were considered suites. The two rooms were connected by a double door in the middle of the wall. Rory went into her room and set her briefcase on the table by the couch and placed her suitcase on the bed, before knocking on the double door.

"It feels like the middle of the night to me and I thought I slept a lot on the plane," Austin yawned.

"Yeah, it's a nine hour time difference, so it is the middle of the night in LA. I need to go take care of a few things. Why don't you get some sleep if you're tired and we can have dinner later?"

"That sounds fine with me."

~ ~ ~

Rory went down to the lobby to take care of the car service arrangements with the concierge and then stopped in the restaurant, where she ate a sweet salmon dish called Gravlax for lunch and ordered a small salad to take up to Austin. She had been surprised to see that Austin had left the separating door on her side unlocked. Rory knocked, walking in when there was no answer. Austin was stretched out in the king size bed under the comforter. She looked incredibly young and innocent, sleeping quietly with a tiny smile on her face. Rory placed the salad and various packages of dressing into the small refrigerator and went back to her room. She made a few calls to the Olympic Village, speaking with different riders and making arrangements to meet with Adler for dinner. Then, she sat down on the couch with her laptop.

Austin woke up an hour later, finding a note on the counter in the small kitchenette. She smiled as she read it.

Austin,

There's a salad in the fridge for you. I wasn't sure which dressing you'd want, so I got as many as I could carry. I'm going to a meeting in an hour, so if I'm not here when you get up I'll be back later for dinner. I would take you with me, but you look peaceful. I hope you slept well. See you soon.

Rory

P.S.

If you need anything call the concierge at the front desk. His name is Mathias. He knows who you are and he has been instructed to get you anything you ask for.

Anything I want...hmm...I could sure think of a few things I'd like to have right now. Austin grinned, shaking her head. She quickly grabbed her salad and walked through the separating door. Rory was sitting on the couch, typing on her computer. Austin was surprised to see her wearing thin-framed glasses.

"Hey," Rory said, smiling.

"Hi, I uh...I didn't know you wore glasses," Austin

said, sitting down next to her.

"Yeah, after the accid—uh over the years my vision has become a little worse, but I only need them for reading, driving at night, things like that. I basically wear them all day around the office though. Are you sure you've never seen me in them? I'm usually wearing them, because I forget to take them off most of the time. I had them on while I was reading on the plane."

"Nope. I must have missed that. I guess I was sleeping. I've never seen them before, but I like them. Do you wear contacts too?"

"Well, thanks I guess, and no. I can't deal with sticking something in my eye. That creeps me out."

"Me too. By the way, I got your note. Thanks for the salad and any kind of vinaigrette dressing is fine." Austin smiled. "I figured I'd see if you had left yet, that's why I came over." *I'm glad to hear that those gorgeous baby blue eyes are natural. I always thought they were.*

"Nope, but I am leaving in a few minutes. Did you want to stay here or go with me?"

"I don't want to get in your way, I'll …"

"You're not in the way, Austin. If you were I wouldn't have brought you with me. I'm meeting with my riders in the Olympic Village where they're staying. This is just a simple meeting to go over their schedules. They're here with team USA, but they're also representing my company, so there are separate photo shoots and other things they need to attend. I also want to see how their equipment is doing. We sent a crate full of extra equipment in case anyone needed anything." Rory closed her computer. "One of my riders is joining us for dinner tonight. She may have her girlfriend with her. I forgot to ask her if she'd arrived yet. Anyway, I hope that doesn't bother you."

"No, not at all."

"The food here is a little strange, but I figured out the menu pretty quickly."

"Sounds good."

"Great! The meeting shouldn't be too long and then we're taking a tour of the venue and snow park with one of the officials. We'll back here in time to scrub up for dinner."

~ ~ ~

The meeting went by quickly and both women had been happy to get back to their rooms and out of the bone chilling cold. Austin walked out onto her balcony, facing a large portion of the snow-covered mountain. Rory was also outside, lounging in a chair, drinking hot chocolate.

"Hey, thanks for the hot chocolate," Austin said, holding up the steaming mug. She'd been surprised when there was a knock on her door and a waiter standing on the other side with the mug.

Rory looked towards the direction of the voice. The moonlight was bright enough for her to make out Austin's silhouette by the rail.

"You're welcome. I had them leave some of the packs behind so that we can make it ourselves next time."

"Good thinking. It's absolutely beautiful here. I never noticed how pretty those mountains were when we arrived this afternoon."

"Yeah, it feels like time's standing still when you look out. I noticed the same thing when I was in Aspen a few weeks ago. The mountain view there is breathtaking too."

They sat in silence, starring out into the moonlit darkness. Each woman wondering what the other was thinking. Rory stood, brushing the snow flurries from her pants.

"I guess we should get going. The driver is probably already here."

Rory stepped into the hall, closing her door. She was surprised to see how much older and grown-up Austin looked when she saw her holding the elevator. She was dressed in jeans with a white sweater and black scarf under a thick leather jacket and snow boots. Her beautiful, honey colored hair hung down in loose waves, all one length and stopping just below her shoulders. She had a few slightly shorter pieces tucked behind one ear. Rory blinked her eyes as her chest tightened and her heart skipped a beat. The more time she spent with Austin, the more her body began to betray her. She'd never felt some of the feelings that had begun to stir deep inside her. It thrilled her and scared the hell out of her at the same time. She wondered for the hundredth time if she was making a huge mistake by getting close to Austin.

Austin smiled, taking in the woman standing in front of her. Rory was also in jeans and snow boots, but she had a black turtleneck on under a gray sweater that had made her eyes even brighter. She had her leather jacket in her hand, slipping into it as she entered the elevator next to Austin.

Her eyes are unbelievable. Austin, you need to get your thoughts in line, girl. She's way too hot for you, and she's straight! Get that one through your thick head before you let the heat spread to places that should remain frozen.

They arrived at the village within a few minutes. Adler came out of the village, escorted by security. She was similarly dressed in jeans and a sweater under a ski jacket with her long curly hair spread out over her shoulders.

"Wow," Austin muttered.

"She's stunning isn't she?" Rory smiled.

"Yeah, and she has a girlfriend?" Austin asked, surprised the beautiful woman walking towards them was a lesbian. She looked like she'd stepped off the cover of a magazine.

"Yes, and she's also one of, if not the, best snowboarders in the world, male or female."

"I've heard her name, Adler something, right?"

"Troy. Adler Troy. She's the new face of my company and a friend of mine," Rory said as she got out. "Is it cold enough for you?" Rory teased.

"Is there snow on the ground?" Adler laughed, half hugging Rory before getting into the vehicle.

Rory climbed in behind her, introducing the women.

"Where's Cason?"

"She's not here yet. She missed her flight because she was held up with an emergency. Hopefully, she will catch the last flight out this evening and arrive in time to see the qualifying tomorrow afternoon."

"Yeah, that sucks."

Adler shrugged. "That's one of the drawbacks of dating a trauma surgeon I guess." She smiled. "I want her with me, but I also love the fact that if she isn't with me, she's saving someone's life."

"That's a good way to look at it," Rory replied.

"So, Austin, do you work at Eden Boards?" Adler

asked, thinking Rory had brought one of the reps with her.

"No." Austin said, shaking her head.

"Austin's one of my mates. She's actually a surfer that is looking to join the tour," Rory exclaimed.

"Cool." Adler nodded. "I surf a little bit when I'm not chasing the snow around the globe, but it's only a hobby. Have you ever been snowboarding?"

"Oh yeah. I'm from North Carolina. We used to go skiing and snowboarding when I was a kid in Sugar Mountain."

"I've been there a couple of times. Our friend here has never been on a snowboard," she said referring to Rory.

"Really?" Austin asked, looking at Rory.

"Yep."

"I think we can rectify that situation while we're here. Don't you?" Austin looked at Adler.

"Oh, sure. Definitely. You can even drop in on the half-pipe if you want," Adler teased.

Rory smiled and shook her head. She had a feeling getting these two together wasn't going to be a good idea.

~ ~ ~

Adler and Austin led the conversation all through dinner, talking about everything from snowboarding and surfing to life and the environment, leaving out the two taboo topics, politics and religion. After dinner, they dropped Adler off at the Olympic Village. Rory climbed out with her.

"A car will be here in the morning to get you and the rest of the riders for the photo shoot for On The Edge magazine. There will also be a photographer at the first practice session of the day, shooting pictures for our website and a few other promotional options."

"Sounds good."

"I'll see you at qualifying or right after that depending on the crowd. Tell Cason I said hello when she gets here."

Adler nodded. "I like her," she winked, nodding in Austin's direction.

"Me too." Rory smiled and got back into the SUV.

As they headed back to the hotel, Austin starred out the window at the snow-covered city streets, wondering why Mathias had been with them the entire evening. He'd sat at a nearby table at dinner and got in and out of the vehicle with them at every stop. She turned towards Rory who was sitting across from her.

"Is he going to be with us the entire time we're here?" Austin asked, tilting her head in Mathias's direction.

Rory smiled. "I had him tag along for security since I was taking one of the Olympians out of the village. Security is tight around team USA."

"I see. Thank you for a wonderful day. I really enjoyed seeing the Olympic Park today, and Adler Troy is pretty cool too."

"You're welcome, mate. I'm glad you had a nice day. I've gotten to know her since I met her in Aspen a few weeks ago. She's fun to be around and she's a damn good snowboarder too! Just wait until tomorrow."

"I'm looking forward to it."

Rory spoke to Mathias briefly, before walking inside the resort behind Austin. The elevator took them swiftly up to their floor and Rory stepped off, peeling her jacket from her shoulders.

"You want some hot chocolate?"

"Sure, can I change first?"

Rory chuckled. "What do you think I'm about to do?" she replied, opening her door. "You can go through my room if you want to."

Austin walked through the separating door and Rory quickly changed into black warm-up pants and a white hooded sweatshirt with her company logo on the front. She made two mugs of hot chocolate and stepped out onto the balcony. Austin stepped outside, walking up to the rail next to Rory. Ironically she was dressed similarly in dark blue warm-up pants and a white Roxy sweatshirt. Rory handed Austin a warm mug, smiling at their similar attire.

"Have you been in my suitcase?" Austin giggled.

"I was about to ask you the same question there, mate."

"Your accent is adorable." *Sexy is more like it, but I know how skittish you are.*

Rory felt her cheeks blush. Luckily, it was dark and Austin couldn't see the shy grin on her face.

"Yeah, yeah. Drink your hot chocolate before it gets cold."

Austin looked up at the stars scattered across the blackened sky.

"Are you going to tell me more about Mathias?"

Rory starred out into the moonlight at the snow covered mountain. "He's my security. Everywhere I go, he goes."

"Why would you need someone following you around?"

"It's not my choice, but I'm learning to deal with it. I get bombarded by the media a lot at the events and I've had some overzealous fans go to the extreme a few times. I've never been hurt or anything like that, but I've encountered some crazy people and asshole journalists that want my story."

"No wonder I was tossed out of your office on my ass. I thought those security guys were nuts!"

Rory laughed. "I know. It's slowed down a lot over the past year and a half though. You didn't see any guards around my houses did you?"

"Uh…no, actually no I didn't see anyone."

"That's because I don't have that kind of problem at home. I used to get bombarded at surf events, which is why I don't go to many of them. Could you imagine if I had told the security guys at my company that you showed up at my house?"

"My God, I'd probably be in jail. Thanks for not ratting me out."

"No worries. I didn't think you were out to get me. Besides, you're harmless and I could take you with my eyes closed," Rory teased.

Austin raised an eyebrow. "Excuse me, I don't think so. We're practically the same size. I'll have you know I could kick your—"

"Okay okay. You look like you want to sucker punch me."

"You're lucky, I almost did," Austin grinned. "I've been laughed at and told I'd never be a pro surfer because of my height."

"Austin, you're not a midget and I've seen surfers shorter than you. You don't have to be six foot tall to surf.

It's all about balance, strength, and mental finesse. I've already told you, you have the skills to be better than anyone on the tour right now and I'm going to help you polish them."

Austin stepped closer, wrapping her arms around Rory's neck. "Thank you," she whispered before walking back inside.

Rory stood out there in the cold a while longer to clear her mind of the way Austin's warm body had felt pressed against her. She didn't want to feel the attraction growing between them and forced herself to forget it existed as she went in for the night.

Realizing she'd forgotten to give Austin the itinerary for the next day of events, Rory knocked on the adjoining door. Austin opened it, dressed in short cotton shorts and a spaghetti strap tank top, leaving nothing to the imagination. Rory was pretty sure there was nothing under either piece of thin clothing. *My God she's bloody trying to kill me! She is so damn cute! And young. She's way too young.*

"I…" Rory stumbled over her words. Clearing her throat, she tried again. "I forgot to give you this. It's for tomorrow, so you know what's going on," she said, staring at Austin's eyes to keep from looking down.

"Oh okay, thanks. Now, I know what time to get up."

"Yeah, I figured that would be helpful. Have a good night. I'll see you in the morning." Rory disappeared quickly.

Chapter Nine

Austin stood in the front section of the crowd, watching the finals for the Women's Superpipe. She was bundled up in a thick, dark blue ski jacket and dark gray ski pants. Her hair was down, with a cotton ski-cap on her head that was pulled down over her ears. She had her gloved hands in her jacket pockets. She cheered for each of the Team USA riders and watched closely as Adler Troy dropped into the pipe, carving back and forth, and flying up out of the pipe into flawless, front-side three-sixties and back-side nines, one right after the other. Austin cheered loudly as Adler slid to a stop at the bottom, spraying a wave of snow over the screaming crowd.

After Adler's first run, Rory rode on the back of an official's snowmobile, down to the spectators at the bottom of the pipe. She was screaming as loud as the rest of the crowd when they posted Adler's scores. She had moved into first place. Each rider still had another run, but it would take perfection to beat Adler's nearly perfect numbers.

Rory knew where Austin was as she made her way through the crowd. She had told her where to stand, figuring that would be the best place for her, versus standing on the side lines at the top of the mountain, where she wouldn't be able to see any of the action. Rory eased up behind the short blond who had an amazingly loud noise coming from her mouth. Seeing Austin's excitement made Rory smile. She put her hands on Austin's shoulders, turning her around. The thick crowd weaved, pushing Austin into Rory as she looked up to see heart-stopping baby blue eyes on her.

"Hey, you!" Austin exclaimed brightly.

"How are you?" Rory smiled, steadying her as the crowd pushed her.

"Great! Those girls are all awesome! Adler was unbelievable! I bet she's going to win gold!"

"Yeah, she looked great! Hey, are you cold? Your nose is red."

"What do you think? I'm a surfer. I live in flip flops, shorts, and a t-shirt."

"No kidding! Do you want to stay here and watch the second runs or go with me?"

"Where are you going?"

"Over to the sidelines for an interview with Adler and Board magazine after the medal ceremony, unless she doesn't win the gold, but it looks like she has it in the bag," Rory said as the second runs started with the first rider falling. "I just came over here to see how you were doing. You don't have to go with me. I'll come get you when I'm finished."

"Are you sure you don't mind?"

"Of course not. I'll bore you death if you hang with

me the whole time. I want you to enjoy yourself." Rory turned to go and bumped into Cason.

"I see you made it."

"Yeah, just in time it looks like! I was held up with a last minute surgery." Cason smiled shaking her head. "I think the gold is hers. I just talked to her and she can barely contain herself."

"Yeah, I bet. Her second run will probably be a victory lap at this point. Hey, I want you to meet someone," Rory replied, grabbing Austin's attention.

"This is my mate, Austin," Rory said. "And this is Dr. Macauley, Adler's girlfriend."

"Oh, hi. It's nice to meet you," Austin replied, shaking her hand.

"Please, call me Cason."

"I'll see you guys in a bit. I need to get ready for that interview," Rory patted Austin on the shoulder before going back through the crowd.

Austin watched her walk away until she could no longer make her out in the crowd.

"How long have you been together?" Cason asked.

"What?" Austin turned back to face her.

"I asked how long you've been together."

Austin shook her head. "We're just friends."

Cason pursed her lips. "All in due time," she said, smiling as she watched the next rider come down the pipe.

"What's that supposed to mean?" Austin raised an eyebrow.

"Anything or nothing. It's depends on how you perceive it."

"I'm a marine biologist, so I'm not the airhead that

you seem to think I am just because I'm a surfer," Austin growled.

Cason looked at the angry young woman staring back at her. *My God, she's like Adler's little sister!* "I'm sorry. We seem to have gotten off on the wrong foot. I didn't mean anything by it and I certainly wasn't insulting your intelligence. I have no idea whether either you have a boyfriend or girlfriend or both. It simply looked to me like you were together. I'm sorry if I've offended you."

"What made you think that? I mean, that we were a couple."

Cason smiled. "It's obvious that she cares for you in the way she looks at you and you...well you light up when she's around. Don't get me wrong, there isn't anything wrong with that."

Austin looked down, kicking the fluffy white snow with her boot. How could a total stranger see right through her?

"She doesn't know does she?" Cason said softly.

"No. I'm pretty sure she's straight anyway," Austin sighed.

"Don't be so sure. These things take time. Not everyone crashes into each other and finds love at first sight." Cason smiled, patting her on the back.

"Is that how you and Adler met?" Austin laughed.

"Oh yeah, she practically knocked me out." Cason grinned. "Long story," she said, shaking her head and watching Adler drop into the half-pipe for her victory lap.

Adler knew she'd won the gold, but threw down a wicked ride full of tricks anyway, showing off her skills all the way down the icy pipe, throwing her hands in the air at the bottom. Her USA teammates bombarded her as she came to a stop, landing like a pile of football players on the ball. She finally scrambled out from under them as the medal podium was being put together at the base of the pipe.

"You're an Olympic Gold Medalist, Adler Troy. How does that feel?" the TV reporter asked.

"I'm stoked! This is unbelievable! I know I wouldn't be standing here right now if it wasn't for two people. My girlfriend, Cason, gives me amazing strength and encouragement and I love her madly for it and Rory Eden for her complete openness in her decision to sponsor me and get me on the best equipment in the world! Also, the girls on team USA have more drive and determination than I've ever seen in anyone. They motivated me more than I ever thought possible."

"Congratulations, Adler. I think they're waiting for you," the reporter said, turning back towards the podium with the silver and bronze medal winners already standing on it.

~ ~ ~

After the medal ceremony and countless other interviews, Rory finally caught back up with Austin. They left the park to have a quiet dinner away from the groups of people that were scattered all over the mountain. Adler and Cason had been invited, but decided to go to one of the resort parties that Rory had also been invited to, instead.

"I know it doesn't look like much, but Mathias mentioned that this place is really good," Rory said as they were seated at a small table.

"This is fine," Austin replied, sitting adjacent to her

at the square table.

Each woman ordered Swedish meatballs since that was the special of the day and had smelled divine when they'd first walked in.

"Did you have a good time today?"

"Oh my God, yes. I think my body became a popsicle about midway through, but I really enjoyed it. Are you sure you don't want to go to that party?"

"Yes. I've had enough of the mobs of people for one day. Besides, I'm definitely not a huge fan of the cold weather either. I'd much rather be in shorts and a t-shirt with sand between my toes," Rory said.

"I knew there was a reason I liked you so much," Austin grinned. "By the way, Cason was interesting to talk to."

"Oh, really? I've talked to her a few times. She and Adler seem really happy together." Rory smiled as the waitress set their drinks on the table.

"Yeah. She thought you and I were together too," Austin said.

"What!" Rory exclaimed, spraying a mouthful of water onto the table.

Austin laughed.

"What did you say to her?" Rory asked, wide-eyed.

"I told her that you and I are just friends. I don't think she believed me though."

"Well, that's absurd. Not every woman in the world is a lesbian," Rory huffed.

Austin shook her head. "Why is this bothering you so much?"

Rory was thankful that their food arrived, interrupting them and stopping her from replying. She wasn't sure what she'd say anyway. Why did it bother

her? She was a lesbian, albeit a closeted one. Still, she wasn't ready to come out, especially to Austin.

"Are you going to answer me?" Austin finally asked, between bites.

"About what?" Rory questioned.

"Why does it bother you so much that Cason thought we were a couple? Surely, you're not homophobic. I mean, you know Adler is out and proud and she's the face of your company. Plus, you seem to know her pretty well."

"It has nothing to do with that and I'm definitely not a homophobe. I just don't like it when people jump to conclusions."

"What if I told you I—"

"How's your food? I think these are the best meatballs I've ever had. Do you need your drink refilled?" Rory cut her off, waving the waitress over. "Can I have a vodka on the rocks with a lime please? Do you want anything?" she said, looking at Austin, who was staring at her with an odd expression on her face and shaking her head no.

"Are you okay?" Austin questioned.

"Yeah, I'm fine," Rory answered.

They spent the rest of their meal in silence. Austin wanted so badly to know why Rory abruptly took offense to the idea of them being a couple. Surely, she wasn't a homophobe. From the mixed signals Austin had been receiving, she was confused as hell about Rory's sexual preference. Maybe Cason was right, all in due time.

~ ~ ~

The next day, they attended the Women's and then the Men's Giant Slalom Finals. Austin stood in the same area that she'd been in the day before, freezing and cheering on the USA riders. She drank more hot chocolate than she ever thought humanly possible and had still been cold down to the bone. Rory had stayed at the top of the hill most of the day, talking with the riders and other sponsors, as well as doing interviews and taking pictures for other countries that had had riders using her equipment.

Austin was intently watching the snowboarders race down through the flags, carving back and force with lightening speed and almost missed her cell phone vibrating in her pocket.

"Hey it's me, what's up?" Lori said as Austin answered.

"Oh my God, you wouldn't believe it if I told you what I was doing right now."

"Hmm….if it involves that hot blond you're hanging with, I'd like to know all of the details."

"Yeah you wish. I'm standing in the front row of the finals for the downhill snowboarding event. It's awesome! They haul ass down this mountain, racing around the flags and carving back and forth."

"Cool, take pictures and send me a postcard."

"I sent one out yesterday, and I'm taking pictures, probably too many."

"I miss you, man. It's been off the wall down in Lunada and Redondo. I was out there with Paul and Shannon yesterday. The sets were almost all overhead!"

"Damn, that sounds tight! We'll hit it up when I get back. Save me some waves."

"Yup, bring me back some snow."

Austin ended the call and watched closely as the last set of male riders came down the hill. Randi Mitchell had already won gold that morning for the women and Stacey Holbritton followed closely behind her with the silver. She watched as the results were displayed on the big screen. Ezekiel Jones had won the men's gold by a fraction of a second. The crowd was roaring with excitement. A few minutes later, the podium was set up and the national anthem was played. Afterwards, Austin spotted Rory standing off to the side with Ezekiel and his coach for a photo.

The mob of spectators began leaving the stands when two guys wearing bright yellow security jackets walked up to Austin. Both spoke to her briefly in English with heavy accents to let her know they were there to escort her safely through the crowd. She saw Rory and Mathias in the direction they were headed, talking to some of the snowboarders.

"Hey, sorry about the goons. I asked them to make sure you made it through the wild people in the stands without being trampled."

"Thanks, they were fine, besides I looked important being escorted through the crowd."

"Well then, Mathias, I think it's time to take Miss Tinsley back to the hotel before her head swells too big for her to get into the car," Rory teased.

Austin playfully slapped Rory's arm as they all walked off laughing.

~ ~ ~

When they arrived back at the hotel, Rory went to

her room. She took her jacket off and checked her watch as she sat lazily on the couch in the living area. *You had better get it over with. There's no time like the present to get your ass chewed out.* She sighed, reaching into her pocket as she pulled out her cell phone. She scrolled through her address book until she found the person she was looking for.

"Well if it isn't Princess Charming," Martie answered.

"Cut the shit, mate. I've had a long day and I really don't have the energy to argue with you."

"Too bad, you deserve to hear it, Rory. Having her there with you is not a good idea at all. People will talk. Are you ready to be outed?"

"Damn it, Martie, I'm not with her like that. We're just friends. Besides she's straight and between the security guy in Aspen and the one I have here, everyone must think I change boyfriends like underwear."

"Ha-ha, I never thought of that. Maybe we should hire one to travel with you on a regular basis."

"Hell no! I've had enough of it and this is only my second trip. The media hasn't been bad at all here. I think people are starting to realize that I'm old news."

"It'll get worse when you start traveling with the Surf Tour. Those are the ones that are out to get you, and for what, I have no idea. But having your little play thing with you really isn't a good idea. Someone will catch on, especially if you take her to surfing events with you."

"I'll deal with that if it happens. I'm just friends with the girl I swear, Martie. She's in her own hotel room and everything. During the last three days, she's been in the stands watching the events, while I've been up on the hill with the officials and our riders."

"Be careful, Rory. You don't need this kind of publicity right now. Eden Boards is taking off faster than we ever imagined it would and we really don't need it to go in that direction. It's bad enough Adler Troy is waving the rainbow flag all over creation. We've received some hate mail since we signed her."

"I know. It's not like I haven't thought about that, Martie, but it's her life and I respect her for living it the way she wants. I'll deal with the repercussions of having Austin around, if it comes to that."

"The fact that you're going to personally train her is enough of a problem without you dragging her halfway across the globe with you."

Rory rubbed her eyes with her free hand. *Trust me, Martie, I know what I'm doing or at least I think I do. There was no way she was going to tell her best friend that she'd developed feelings for the young surfer. She'd just have to learn to control them.* She finished her call and walked over to the door to Austin's room, knocking softly. Austin answered, wearing a small t-shirt that barely touched the top of her thin jogging pants, allowing the tanned skin of her stomach to play peek a boo when she moved. Her hair was pulled up off her neck with a clip. Rory's chest tightened and she was unsteady on her feet as her temperature rose drastically. Sweat began to bead up on her brow.

Austin looked quizzically at Rory who was still dressed in her heavy clothing and shoes.

"Hey."

"Were you sleeping?" Rory asked.

"No, I was just watching TV and talking to Lori on the phone. Did you go somewhere else?"

"No, why?"

"You've got to be uncomfortable and you look really hot."

Rory laughed. It hadn't occurred to her that she'd forgotten to change out of her heavy snow clothing. "Yeah, I guess I am getting a little warm. I just got off the phone with my office, so I haven't changed yet. I'm assuming you don't want to go to dinner since you've obviously gotten comfortable."

"I was hoping we could order room service or if you're going out to eat, then I'll just order it myself. I think I've had enough cold for the day. I need to thaw out."

"That's fine. I'll go change and we can eat together if you want, unless you want to be alone."

"No, of course not," Austin smiled.

"Order whatever you think sounds good. See you in a few minutes," she said, backing out of the room.

Rory was overheated and sweating profusely as she peeled out of her snow pants and turtleneck. She took a quick shower to rinse off the sweat and cool her core. She pulled on a t-shirt and sweatpants and towel dried her short hair. Austin was lying on the couch watching TV when she walked back into the room.

"I snuck into your room while you were in the shower," Austin said, nodding towards the two steaming cups of hot chocolate on the table.

Rory reached for one and walked over to the sliding glass doors for the balcony. "It's snowing again," she said.

"Yeah, I noticed. It's so beautiful here." Austin walked over, standing next to her. "Everything is so pristine and untouched."

"I think the moon looks bigger here. I guess it's because of the mountains and the snow, but it just looks closer to me. The stars seem brighter too," Rory said, sipping from the warm mug in her hand.

"Maybe you're just seeing things differently now," Austin murmured.

Rory shrugged. "I have a meeting in the morning and then I'll be back around ten to get you. Dress really warm."

"Cool, where are we going?"

"Just be ready to go at ten or you'll be pissed at yourself, trust me," Rory said as the waiter arrived with their dinner.

Chapter Ten

Rory awoke the next morning and dressed in the warmest clothes she had packed. After a quick cup of hot chocolate to warm her even further, she figured it was time to inform Austin of her plans for the day. The door opened as she reached out to knock, startling both women.

Rory shrieked and Austin nearly smacked her.

"Jesus, Rory!"

"Well I wasn't expecting you to open the bloody door before I knocked."

"You scared the shit out of me."

"I'm sorry. You scared me too."

"Are you going to tell me where we're headed?"

"Actually, that's why I was coming over. We're going snowboarding. That is unless…"

Austin couldn't believe her ears. "No way!"

"Is that okay with you?"

"I could kiss you, Rory Eden. Yes! Yes, it's okay with me," Austin gleamed.

"Calm down." Rory laughed. "Come on. Let's get going before they rent out our equipment."

~ ~ ~

It was a few degrees below zero outside. Rory pulled her ski cap down and tucked her ears up under it. *Eden, you can do this you chicken shit! It'll be fine; it's a snowboard on top of snow-covered solid ground. Get your head out of your ass before you make a fool of yourself in front of her...*"Okay okay, leave me alone. I can do this. I'll just close my eyes and hold my breath. That's just great, stupid, you'll run into a tree and kill yourself. Here they come—it's too late to talk yourself out of it now. God, just let me get through this. Please!" *Piece of cake. If I could surf fifteen foot Pipeline waves with no fear, I sure as shit better be able to ride a dinky little board down a mountain. Bloody hell!* Rory paced in the snow next to her board.

Austin had stopped off for one last bathroom break while Rory secured lessons with the private instructor and went in search of the additional equipment that Rory's company had sent for their sponsored riders to make sure it was available for their use for the day. Austin examined all of the gear as she walked up. Rory stood off to the side, still invisibly fighting with her conscience.

"Are you okay?" Austin asked, raising an eyebrow.

"Yeah. Fine. You?" Rory buzzed around like she was on speed.

Austin laughed.

Their tall, dark-haired private instructor walked up before Austin could reply. She had a thick Italian accent, but she spoke perfect English. "Let's get you girls ready to tackle this mountain. Shall we?"

"That's a lot of stuff," Austin said.

"Yes, but when you fall you'll be glad you had this stuff on. Oh and trust me, you will fall."

"That's just great to know." Rory stepped into the conversation. "Hi, I'm Rory Eden, and this is Austin Tinsley. Mathias highly recommended you to me."

"Ah, Mathias. He's a good guy," she said, smiling. "I'm Nikkola Franchino."

"Yes, he's been very helpful so far. It's nice to meet you, Miss Franchino," Rory said, shaking her hand.

"Welcome to Stockholm and please call me Nikki. It's very nice to finally meet you. I am a huge fan of yours and I actually ride one of your boards, as well as use your boots and bindings. You make great equipment. I see that you've brought your own equipment with you. It's much better than the rental stuff," she whispered with a smile. "So, how often do you snowboard, Ms. Eden?" she asked.

Austin stood back with her eyebrows furled together, watching the dark-haired woman flirt carelessly with Rory. "I used to go every year," Austin replied, glaring at the woman.

"Please, call me Rory, and I hate to say it, but I've never learned to snowboard. One of my sponsored riders keeps promising to take me out on the snow, but she's busy winning gold medals." Rory smiled. "I actually haven't ridden one of my surfboards either. I spend too much time in an office these days." Rory smiled again.

"Great, I'm glad I can be the first person to teach you to snowboard. Believe me, if you can carve snow like you rip waves, you'll pick this up pretty easily. Are there any questions before we get started?"

Rory and Austin looked at each other and then back at Nikki, shaking their heads. Austin's blood was boiling. She couldn't believe the boldness of the woman flirting with Rory and the way Rory was eating it up made her sick in her stomach.

"Okay, here is your board and your boots. Make sure your pant legs are on the outside and then close your boots up tightly. They're a little funny to walk in at first, but you'll get used to it," Nikki said, watching Rory get her gear on. "Put your helmet on over your ski cap and snap the buckles together under your chin and put your goggles on your helmet so that you can slide them down over your eyes easily."

"I had forgotten how much crap you have to wear. I definitely prefer surfing. At least I can wear a bathing suit or a wet suit and be fine. I feel like I weigh over two-hundred pounds with all of this shit on."

Rory shook her head, laughing at Austin. *I guess I can't say anything. How would my riders feel if they found out I complained the entire time? Forget about wearing all of this shit, I'll be doing good to make it to the bottom of the mountain.*

"Now before you strap onto the boards there are a few basic moves I want to show you. Before anything, you need to learn how to stop. Basically, you turn so that you're facing forward rather than the side and lean back so that the edge of the backside of the board catches the snow. This will slow you to a stop." Nikki strapped on her board and began showing them each move as she explained it.

"Whatever you do, don't lean forward or you'll plant

head first into the snow and barrel roll. The second thing is how to turn and maneuver around obstacles that might be in your way. This is called carving and basically it's similar to the way you carve on a surfboard, except your weight is almost evenly distributed on a snowboard instead of on your back foot like on a surfboard. You lean in or out with your body so that you're carving the snow with the front side or backside edge of the board. A small trick that you can do is called a tail-wheelie. This is where you put your weight on the back foot and the front of the board comes up. Once you get the hang of this, you can rotate one-hundred and eighty degrees and ride fakie. This similar to the way you would do it on a surfboard, which is basically with your other foot out front. After you learn that trick, we'll go up on the lift and go down one of the trails. Are you guys ready?"

"Hell yeah!" Austin jumped up. It had been a couple of years since she'd been on a snowboard, but everything had started coming back to her. She looked over at Rory who was standing stiffly with her eyes bugging out of her head.

"I guess I'm as ready as I'll ever be," Rory said, swallowing the lump in her throat. *You can do this. Relax.*

Nikki showed Rory how to attach her boots to the bindings and snap them in place as Austin moved around on her board, getting used to the feeling again.

When everyone was ready, Austin led the way down the little bunny hill with Rory behind her. Nikki rode close to Rory, allowing her to mimic the instructor's movements.

Snowboarding had come back to Austin pretty rapidly. She was carving back and forth until she leaned too far and fell backwards. She stood up laughing, brushed the snow off, and kept going down the small hill. She leaned back on her left foot, riding a few tail-wheelies and midways down the hill she tried to rotate and ride fakie, wiping out twice before finally completing the trick.

Rory was surprised at herself and amazed to see how similar snowboarding was to surfing. She carved back and forth down the hill, doing tail-wheelies and riding fakie with no problem. She fell a few times, but after the initial shock of the first fall and realizing she was okay, she'd gotten back up and kept going.

"It looks like you have it down. Let's take the lift up and see how you do on a trail," Nikki said.

Rory and Austin followed her over to the ski lift. As the chair came around, all three women squished in with Rory in the middle. The bone-chilling wind was like nothing Rory had ever experienced. She huddled into her jacket like a turtle in a shell as the chair moved further and further up the mountain.

They finally arrived at their destination, hoping off and riding their boards out of the way.

"This trail over here to the left is sort of a beginner and intermediate trail, so you won't have any obstacles to go around like trees or rocks. You two go in front of me and remember to watch your lines and to look back before turning. Sometimes skiers come by and they will crash into you. I'll go behind you both," Nikki exclaimed, pulling her goggles over her eyes.

Austin went first, followed by Rory. They carved back and forth down the mountain doing the simple tricks here and there. Both women's exceptional balance and surfing skills showed as they maneuvered down the mountain. As she became more comfortable with the board, Rory began ducking down, carving fast to the right and dragging her left hand in the snow as she turned quickly back to the left. Then, she spun around to ride fakie and do the same trick over again with the opposite hand in the snow.

Nikki watched the former surf champion as she rode back and forth with the agility of an athlete.

At the base of the mountain, Austin was stoked and ready to go again and Rory was shocked to see how she'd immediately taken to the board. She hadn't surfed in over four years, yet her balance and skills had easily come back to her.

"Shall we go again, ladies?" Nikki asked.

~ ~ ~

Austin and Rory spent the rest of the day riding different courses and learning new tricks. When the sun finally went down, they headed over to the lodge to sit by the fire in the lobby and warm up.

"Rory, I had no idea you could ride a snowboard like that. You impressed me today." Austin smiled.

"I guess it comes naturally. I had a great time," Rory replied, smiling back.

"You both looked good out there on the mountain today. I wish the other slope had been groomed. I'd like to see what you can do on the lift-off," Nikki teased, talking about the large jump on the other course that had been closed due to the Olympic Games.

"Oh no! I don't think I want to go flying through the air," Rory said, shaking her head.

Nikki reached over, placing her hand on Rory's knee. "There's no need to get nervous." Nikki winked.

Austin wanted to killer her when she saw Nikki put her hand on Rory. She envisioned herself literally strangling the exotic woman, making her choke on her own accent.

Nikki wasn't sure what was going on between Austin and Rory, but she could see the possessive look Austin was giving her. *So, you think she's yours, do you? We'll see about that.*

"I'm heading over to the local tavern for a drink. Rory, would you like to join me? I'm sure some of the locals would like to meet you."

"Uh...I probably shouldn't. I have some work to catch up on. Maybe another time." *Nonchalant, no-strings sex is probably not what I need right now. At least not with you.*

"Suit yourself. Here's my cell number if you change your mind." She kissed Rory on the cheek and handed her a business card. "Goodnight, Miss Tinsley." Nikki grinned at her as she walked by.

Rory and Austin stepped into the elevator. Austin pressed the number for their floor, smacking the panel when the number didn't light up.

"Easy, mate. What's gotten your feathers all ruffled?" Rory asked, reaching around her and pressing the button for their floor.

"You tell me?!" Austin growled.

Rory stared at her as the elevator ascended, wondering what she was talking about. She'd never seen Austin angry and she wasn't even sure this was anger. Austin looked more like she was ready to bolt as soon as doors opened. "I'm not sure what's bothering you, but…are you ready to go home? Is that what it is?"

Austin wanted to smack her upside her cute head. "Seriously?" she huffed, shaking her head, then crossing and uncrossing her arms. Finally, she turned to face Rory head on. "What does she have that I don't, besides big boobs and a ridiculous accent?"

"What? Who?" Rory asked, confused.

"Nikki or Nikola or whatever the fuck her name was," Austin spat as the doors opened. "Never mind, I'm going to bed," she said as she walked away.

"Wait." Rory bolted out of the elevator, stopping at Austin's door. "I'm not sure what's going on here, but we need to talk about this."

"There's nothing to talk about, Rory." Austin put her keycard in the door, pushing the handle as it unlocked. "Nothing at all," she whispered as she went inside, closing the heavy door behind her.

"Shit!" Rory growled to the empty hallway.

This had been the last thing Rory had expected. Knowing she'd developed feelings for Austin was one thing. She could easily hide the growing attraction, but the fact that Austin was possibly feeling the same way was not good. Not good at all. She couldn't handle being that close to Austin, separated by a thin wall, and not talking to each other. She walked back to the elevator, pushing the button for the lobby. She felt the business card Nikki had given her when she slipped her hands into her pockets. It would be so easy to spend the night using her to forget about the blond upstairs, but nothing in the world would permanently remove Austin from her mind or her heart and that scared Rory. It scared her more than the idea of surfing again.

"You want to know what she has that you don't, Austin? Nothing. She has nothing and you have everything," she whispered as the elevator stopped.

Rory thought about calling Martie as she sat down at the bar, ordering a whiskey on the rocks, but thought better of it. If Martie knew about her feelings for Austin, she'd flip out. Hell, she barely knew about the feelings herself. How the hell would she explain them to anyone else? She'd only ever loved one other person in her life and Martie had turned out to be more like a sister and a best friend than a girlfriend. She'd spent most of her life chasing pipe dreams and double over-head waves. Those two things had left very little room for anything else and Martie had always filled the companionship void. Austin had somehow found the tiny crack in Rory's perfectly molded life and squeezed herself through it, into the little space that made Rory's pulse race and her heart skip a beat.

Rory drank a long sip of the stiff drink. *Austin doesn't need the baggage of a washed up, old sock that's afraid of the water. She deserves so much more.*

~ ~ ~

"It's a shame we're leaving today. I was beginning to really enjoy this place," Austin said as she took her seat on the plane. *I was getting used to being around you all day, every day. Maybe going home is a good thing. I think I need some time away from you to clear my head.*

"Yeah, it's beautiful here, but personally I'm freezing my ass off and I'm ready to go home." Rory smiled. She was glad Austin hadn't mentioned the events of the night before. She just wanted to get back to California where they would have a lot more distance between them than a paper thin wall and an unlocked door. She still wasn't sure how to talk about what was going on between them and she was glad Austin hadn't brought it up either.

"What's on your schedule when you get back?"

"Uh...I believe the Gold Coast Pro in Australia is the next thing on the calendar. It's the first stop on the Championship Tour for this year."

"Oh wow, so you get to see your family..."

"I'm not sure what I'm going to do yet, I haven't decided if I'm going. This is just the next event on the calendar."

"I see."

"When we get back, I want you in the water the next day. I'll try to come watch you once or twice this week if I can."

"No problem, Lori's already talking about going down to Redondo."

"Make sure you don't overdo it. I'm sure you'll be tired."

"Yes ma'am," Austin teased.

~ ~ ~

Rory awoke to her cell phone ringing on her night stand. "Noon! Holy shit!" she screeched, looking at the alarm clock. She was glad she had taken the day off to rest before going back to the office.

"I'm glad to see you're back on U.S. soil. Want to join me for dinner tonight?" Martie asked when she answered.

"Nah. Hey, Martie, on second thought, why don't you

come here for dinner? You can bring me a six pack."

"Alright, I'll be by around seven."

"Is Martina Cruz working late? No way!" Rory teased.

"Cut the shit, you know someone has to run this place while you're out gallivanting all over the world."

"Gallivanting for a good cause, mate!"

"Ha-ha, yeah, I'll be there shortly."

~ ~ ~

Rory sat back in the wooden Adirondack chair on the deck, listening to the waves crashing against the shore. Martie was next to her, doing her best to keep up with Rory, who was already on her fourth bottle of beer.

"I can't believe you still drink this shit."

"What shit?"

"Beer," Martie grimaced.

"Mate, you know I have liquor. Go look in the bar. I didn't tell you that you *had* to drink beer. I just figured you could supply it." Rory smiled.

"You're hopeless." Martie laughed and went inside. She returned a few minutes later with a Margarita.

"You look much better with that, or a Corona. I always thought you looked sexy drinking Corona when we were younger in La Jolla." *I must be drunk.* Rory thought.

Martie laughed. "Yeah and I remember how much you bitched about ruining the beer when we made you put a lime in it."

"Yeah, well that just doesn't make any sense to me. We wound up drinking Tequila, anyway. Man, those were crazy days." Rory laughed, shaking her head.

"I might as well get it out while I can. Happy Birthday, Rory."

"Oh, mate, you know I hate my birthday."

"We need to celebrate."

"What's there to celebrate? So I'm another year older, my God can you believe I'm thirty? I'll be forty before you know it and I'm already a washed-up old sock!"

"Give me a break. I'm only a year younger than you!" Martie walked into the house, returning with two small boxes.

"What's this?"

"This one is from the office, and the other one's from me."

"You guys really shouldn't have done this."

"Just open the damn boxes, Rory." Martie growled at her best friend.

Rory opened the box from her staff first. It contained a two inch long Swarovski Crystal snowboard.

"Wow, this is beautiful." Rory already knew right where she'd put it.

She opened the other box which was similar in size and found a matching crystal surfboard. She was speechless as a small tear escaped her eye. Martie was the only person who really knew what surfing had meant to her. "I...God, Martie, thank you...this..."

"I know," Martie said, taking a deep breath and wrapping her arms around her friend. The past four years had been turmoil for her too, watching her best friend almost die, and then watching the agony in Rory's light blue eyes every single day had torn her apart.

Rory wiped her face and walked into the house. She put both figurines in the corner curio in her study. She'd started a small crystal collection over the past year and had already had three pieces in the case.

"Okay, enough birthday drama. So what's going on, Rory? You still haven't told me about Sweden," Martie said as Rory walked back out onto the deck.

Rory looked at her oddly, knowing damn good and well what she was talking about. "Nothing happened. We watched the games, spent some time with Adler and I signed autographs and went through a hundred interviews."

"Uh huh…"

"We went snowboarding."

"Snowboarding!" Martie practically yelled.

"Yeah."

"You, the person who won't go anywhere near any kind of board at all? It's bad enough that after all of this time, three God damn years, Rory, you decide to go back to the ocean, for her, with her, and now you're been snowboarding too! What's gotten into you?"

"Calm down, Martie. It's not what you think it is."

"The fucking hell it isn't! What are you doing with her, Rory?"

"Nothing. That's just it. I swear, Martie. I haven't been surfing and have no desire to ever go back in the water. I go and watch her and give her pointers. Snowboarding was, well…I don't…all I know is, you can't crack your head on a reef or drown in the God damn snow! I was scared, but I felt safe, so I did it! Bloody hell, I wish you'd just let it go and trust me."

"I'm trying really hard here, Rory. Really fucking hard."

"I'm sorry," Rory said, pacing the deck.

"Why are you sorry?"

"Hell I don't know…what do you want me to say?"

"Are you in love with her?"

"What? No! Martie, this has nothing to do with Austin."

"Well I'm just trying to figure out why you're doing the things you're doing all of a sudden. Something changed in you and it happened when you started hanging around her."

"I'm friends with her and that is all! She's only twenty one, for God's sake. You know me better than that."

"I thought I did." Martie said angrily. She was mad at her best friend, but she was angrier at the fact that Rory was slowly letting the barrier down that she'd built around herself after the accident and Martie wasn't the one at her side. Some young, wannabe surfer had slipped in, taking her place and this girl has no idea the kind of power she has over Rory. Martie didn't want to see her best friend get hurt.

"Martie, come on," Rory replied, sitting back down next to her.

"What now?"

"Huh?"

"What happens now? Where do you go from here?"

Rory blew out a long breath. "I'm meeting her at Redondo, Tuesday morning."

"Great." Martie irritably changed the subject. "You know Angel knows your schedule. She's expecting you next week."

"I'm going to Vermont."

"Don't you think you need to be at the first event of the surf season?"

"No."

"Besides, we're sending the ski reps to Vermont. Coming off our performance at the Olympics, we'll be busy with retail sales. There's no need for you to be there."

"Well, send the surf reps to Australia then."

"Damn it, Rory, I'm so tired of being the fence between you and your mother. She knows when the big surfing events are being held in Australia and she also knows you will more than likely be there because your company makes the best damn surfboard in the world. You two need to work out your differences. I can't be the go to anymore. I won't be."

"I don't have anything to say to her, Martie."

"Well, she obviously has something to say to you. Did you even answer her call today?"

"Yeah, Uncle Mick cornered me on the phone and she was with him."

"Good. You need to hear her out, Rory. You only have one mother."

"Bloody hell!" Rory spat.

"Does that mean you're going to Oz?"

"Fine. Have Alex book it. I'm not promising that I'll even see, Angel. Uncle Mick keeps calling me and threatening to come here and drag me out of the office if he doesn't see me soon."

"Good for him. At least call her while you're there."

"No promises."

"Okay. I guess you going there is good enough."

"Make it for two." Rory said, opening another beer.

"What was that?" Martie asked with a raised eyebrow.

"Two. Tell her to make the arrangements for two people."

"You're not, no Rory. You don't need to take her home with you."

"You, dingo. I want you to go with me."

"Me? Who would stay here and run the office? Besides, I don't want to be anywhere near Angelina Zane when she finds out you're in Australia and didn't even talk to her. Hell no!" Martie shook her head frantically.

"You puss! Fine, I'll go alone." *Hmm...maybe I could take Austin. She could surf some real waves. Now, there's a thought.*

"What are you thinking?" Martie questioned. She saw the look in Rory's eyes.

"Nothing. I wasn't thinking anything."

"Sure, and I'm straight," Martie laughed.

~ ~ ~

Rory sat in the comfortable leather chair behind her large desk, staring at the framed magazine covers and articles about her that covered one wall of her office. Her college degrees hung neatly alongside them in cherry colored wooden frames. Both of those times in her life seemed so long ago, almost like they had happened in another lifetime. She checked the time on her watch and pressed the button on the intercom.

"Yes, Rory?"

"Alex, send my calls to Martie. I'm stepping out for awhile. I may not be back today."

"Yes ma'am."

Rory dialed another extension on the intercom.

"Yes?"

164

"You're taking my calls for the rest of the day."

"What? Why? Who are you hiding from…oh no you don't, Rory. Your mother calls me enough as it is!"

"Huh? I'm not talking about, Angel. I'm going to Redondo with Austin and I don't know what time I'll be finished. I told Alex to send you my calls. I may not be back in today."

"Gee thanks. I get to run the office while the boss goes to play with her new little 'girl toy'!"

"Martie, I'm going to pretend I never heard you say that. I thought you understood," she said, ending the call.

~ ~ ~

There's no need to be nervous. Why be nervous? This is absurd! Rory drove home and changed into thin nylon pants and a t-shirt with her company logo on it. She stepped into her flip flops and grabbed a thin jacket on her way out.

Rory turned into the familiar parking lot and was able to get the last open parking spot. She quickly put the top up on her little sports car and stepped out. She found Austin watching her from the walkway leading down to the beach. She was standing by the steps with the top of her wetsuit hanging down by her waist and a white and purple skin-tight rash guard covering her upper body. She held her board loosely under her left arm.

"Hi!"

"Hey. How's it going?" Rory asked.

Better now, I guess. I don't know, Maybe this isn't a good idea after all. "Fine. I've been watching the lines for about twenty minutes. The sets look nice and tight with a few flat ones here and there."

"Let's see if you've still got it!" Rory smiled, patting her on the shoulder as she walked past her down to the sand. She kept her eyes on the line, watching every wave as it began, rose, crested, and fell. They stopped walking close to the tidal line and Austin pulled the top of her wetsuit up.

Rory watched Austin paddle out and sit on her board. *Wait for it, wait for it, wait for it...there!* "Go! Go!" she shouted. *That-a-girl!*

Austin paddled into the perfect wave, popping up quickly and dropping in one fluid motion. She wasted no time ripping back and forth into a tail-slide. The wave flattened before she could get any further.

"God damn it!" she spat as she paddled back to the line. "Come on, Tinsley. You've got this! Damn flat fucking waves!" Another set of waves came rippling by. *Wait, wait, yeah baby!* The next wave in the set promised to crest nicely as she paddled into it.

Austin immediately ripped back and forth a few times to gain speed on the small wave and flew off the top into a nose-grab aerial. Landing perfectly, she moved directly into another amazing trick before her wave flattened again. She climbed back up on the board cursing and spitting saltwater. Rory could see the frustration from her position on the beach.

She needs more time. She can't get going on these baby waves. Rory waved, calling her back in. That was it. She knew what she had to do. The decision had been made. Austin walked up to her, shrugging the top of her wetsuit down. The wet rash guard clung to her upper body like a second layer of skin, leaving nothing to the imagination. *Damn! Don't look, don't look! Have mercy!*

Catch your breath, stupid, before you pass out.

Austin threw the towel around her shoulders."I can't believe these shitty waves," she said, raising an eyebrow when she saw the look on Rory's face. "Are you okay?"

"Yeah. Great." Rory scratched her head. "Don't let it get to you. It takes a lot of finesse to ride these little waves like they're perfect sets. You need to be ready for them though. You never know what you're going to be faced with in a competition and especially in the qualifiers. You'll see bigger waves in your bathtub sometimes."

"This sucks." Austin hung her head down, toweling her hair before slinging it back over her shoulders in a gesture that completely derailed Rory's train of thought.

"Uh…no, it's uh…no." Rory said.

Austin laughed. "What?"

"Didn't you ask me something?"

"No," Austin laughed again, pulling her wetsuit completely off, revealing her tiny black bikini bottoms. "I said these waves suck."

Good God, she's trying to kill me. Rory walked a few feet away, trying to get her thoughts under control. She couldn't remember every feeling so aroused just by looking at someone. "This is crazy," she whispered.

"Huh?" Austin asked, slipping shorts over her bottoms. She peeled her rash guard off, revealing a black string bikini top and reached down into her bag, pulling out a long sleeved t-shirt that she slid over her head.

"I think I'm going crazy," Rory said, staring out at the waves as she began walking away.

"Uh…okay?" Austin followed Rory back to the parking lot.

"How are your grades?" Rory removed her eye glasses to wipe off a smudge.

"My...oh school...fine, I have an exam tomorrow then nothing major until I have my finals in a few weeks. Why?" Austin replied, putting her bag in her truck.

"I told you this isn't going to interfere with school. How did you handle your studies while we were in Sweden?"

"I was fine. I made sure I studied and emailed my quizzes."

"I know. I saw you."

"Okay? I met with an academic advisor in student affairs a few days ago and as long as I pass my finals next month, I'll graduate this term."

"Wow, that's great! I'm going home next week and as crazy as it sounds, I want to take you with me, but not if it will interfere with school. That's more important."

"What?" Austin was confused.

"I think it will benefit you to see a pro competition and actually surf pro-style waves. I need to see if you can handle it, and I really want to see what you can do with a real wave. We will only be there a few days so we'll have to work on finesse another time, but at least this will give me somewhere to start with you. I can't tell shit with these Mickey Mouse waves."

"Rory, I still don't understand what you're talking about." Austin strapped her board to the rack on her SUV.

"Oh, I'm sorry. I mean Australia."

"What?" Austin shrieked. Her wet foot slipped on the running board, causing her to fall back into Rory's arms.

Rory reacted quickly, wrapping her arms around Austin and setting her down on her feet. She hesitated before letting go. "Don't break your neck on my account." Rory smiled. "Anyway, the Gold Coast Pro is there next week and I need to make an appearance since this is the first stop on the tour."

"Wow!" Austin threw her arms around Rory's neck. Rory moved to back away, but put her arms around Austin's slim waist, holding the smaller woman against her.

"I'm sorry, I guess I got a little excited," Austin beamed, pulling away from her. "Of course I want to go. Are you kidding me?! Don't worry about school. It'll be fine."

"Yeah, okay…well, I need to go. We're leaving on Monday night, so I'll pick you up at five p.m." Rory walked around to the driver's side of her car, sliding down into the black leather seat of her Audi. Austin watched her drive away.

"Australia baby! Yes!" she shouted.

~ ~ ~

Austin almost knocked her roommate over as she stormed into the apartment. "Lori! Lori, where are you?"

"I'm right here," she said moving the door that had just about knocked her out.

"Oh hey, guess what, you'll never believe this."

Lori kicked her flip flops off and sat on the couch. *So much for going to the library.* "What's up? Let me guess, Surfer Barbie kissed you."

"She asked me to go home with her."

"Okay? Did you? Oh my God, you had sex with her!"

"No, no. Australia. She wants me to go to Australia with her next week."

"What the hell?"

"That's what I said. At first, I thought she was going to tell me to forget all of this. Oh my God Redondo totally failed me today. You wouldn't believe it. I couldn't get a ride to save my ass."

"That sucks, but what brought up the idea of you going with her? And what the hell for?"

"She's going for the Gold Coast Pro. She wants me to see how the pro comp's work and she said she wants to see what I can do on a real wave."

"Wow. That's uh…interesting. I still can't believe you're friends with this woman. She just took you to Sweden for the Olympics, and now Australia. Are you sure you're not sleeping with her?"

"Yes! I promise I'm not. She's...I…" her mind drifted back to Sweden when she'd almost let her feelings ruin everything.

Lori sighed. "She's going to break your heart."

Chapter Eleven

Rory killed a Mimosa as soon as the flight had taken off. Three hours into the fifteen hour flight to Sydney, she had been reading the latest issue of On The Edge magazine when she'd felt Austin's head hit her right shoulder. The small blond had been asleep for the better part of an hour. *Great.* She stared out the window of the large airliner.

Austin finally woke an hour and a half later with her head still on Rory's shoulder.

"Sorry," she said, grinning sheepishly.

"No problem."

Their long journey finally ended when their second flight brought them to the Gold Coast, landing with a jolting thud on the tarmac. Rory stretched her neck, sighing as she looked out the window. She grabbed Austin's hand as they exited the jet so that she could keep up with the smaller woman in the herd of people in the airport. Rory lead them over to the baggage claim area.

"Stay right here. I'll be right back," Rory said.

"Where are you going?"

"To find the security guard my company hired. He may be outside waiting." *I hate being babysat, but it's even worse when I have to find the idiot.*

Austin stood still, watching people come and go. Five minutes later, Rory returned, alone.

"No security?"

"Nope. I guess not. I swear I'm tired of chasing these fruit loops. Bloody hell."

"Bloody hell what, you ankle-biter!" The deep voice startled Austin and Rory turned into the outstretched arms of her uncle.

"Uncle Mick!" she squeal as he picked her up off the ground.

"What's got you mad as a cut snake? You look like you're ready to wallop someone."

"Yeah, my security guard. What did you do with him?"

"Angelina Zane's daughter was coming home for the first time in nearly five years. Did you think she was going to let some useless dingo's donger protect you?!"

Rory laughed. Austin was surprised at how similar Rory was to the man. They didn't look much alike, but their mannerisms were almost identical. She didn't however, understand a word the man was saying.

"Who's the Sheila?" he asked, turning towards Austin.

"This is my mate, Austin Tinsley. Austin this old bloke is my uncle, Mickel Zane."

"She's a beaut! Is this the ankle-biter you told me about?"

Rory grinned.

He extended his hand. "Please call me Mick."

Austin shook his hand and smiled.

"Your mum's waiting at the house. You know she's expecting you to stay with her while you're home."

"That figures. How is the old rat bag anyway?"

"Steady on. Rory, do your uncle a solid and chew the fat before you shoot through. She's your mum and you only get one of them."

"Yeah yeah, take me to her I guess. I'm not promising that we'll stay there," she said.

Rory put her hand in the small of Austin's back, urging her to follow Mick. Austin jumped at the light touch. Rory bent close to her ear, whispering, "Be prepared. We're headed to the family house. My mother is expecting us to stay there, well me at least. She doesn't know about you, yet. Anyway, it won't be too bad. She won't battle with me in front of you, but just be prepared. She can be a real bitch sometimes. I've never…I mean…she may act a little weird around you."

"Great." Austin grinned.

"I'll get us out of there and into the hotel we were supposed to be staying at," she continued.

Mick walked them towards the waiting limo. The driver immediately stepped towards Rory. "Welcome home, Rory."

Rory smiled, "Hello, Bob."

~ ~ ~

Austin watched through the dark window as the city went by. They drove for nearly half an hour before she saw the gorgeous mansion up on top of a hill, completely surrounded by an iron gate with a lot of trees and shrubs.

173

As they pulled around the u-shaped driveway, she noticed large columns on either side of the entry way, leading to the double front door.

Rory took a deep breath as she climbed out of the car. "Here we go," she sighed.

Bob carried their bags inside, setting them in the foyer. Austin followed Rory and Mick through the doorway. She was amazed at the vast amount of artwork covering the beige and crème colored walls. The floor was covered in large white tiles. They'd barely stepped inside when a short, plump woman came running up to them.

"Rory, welcome home."

Rory smiled, hugging the woman. "Thanks, Matilda."

"Oh and who do we have here?" Matilda asked.

"God my manners, I swear I left them over the ditch. I'm sorry. Austin, this is Matilda. She's my mother's housekeeper. Bob, the driver, is also the butler and Matilda's husband. They live in the guesthouse on the other side of the property. They've been working for my family as long as I can remember. Matilda, this is my mate, Austin Tinsley."

Austin smiled and felt Rory stiffen next to her as she looked up to see one of the most elegant looking women she'd ever seen, walking down the long winding staircase. She was wearing black slacks and a white blouse and had shoulder length brown hair. Austin could definitely tell the woman was related to Rory. She was attractive, with a slender build and she was just about Rory's height. She stepped off the staircase and onto the tile. Austin noticed her eyes were green instead of baby blue like Rory's.

"Step aside, Matilda. Let me see my daughter."

174

Angel walked up to Rory, stopping to look deep into her eyes. *My God, she looks just like you Randall.* "Hello, Rory."

"Hello, Mum." Rory said inwardly, trying desperately to play nice

Angel bent forward, wrapping her arms around her daughter's shoulders, before quickly stepping back. Rory barely returned the embrace. Austin felt the coldness in the room and she was sure it wasn't because of the air conditioner.

Angel raised an eyebrow, giving Austin a quizzical look. "Who's the yank?" she said, stepping around her daughter. Rory countered her, stepping closer to Austin.

"This is my mate, Austin Tinsley. Austin, this is my mother, Angelina Zane."

Austin stepped forward, offering her hand, which Angel shook politely.

"Please, call me Angel." She smiled, giving Austin a once over. *I have no idea why you're standing in my house, but I will get to the bottom of it. Trust me.* "Martie didn't cross the pond? I figured your best mate would be with you."

"She was busy." *Although, I wish she was here.*

"Well, stop mobbing around the door and move into the lounge," Angel said, shooing everyone into the living room. "Bob, run those bags upstairs please."

Rory rubbed her temples. *I'm so in the shit!* "I wasn't planning on staying at the house."

"You always stay at the family home when you are visiting. I'll not have it any other way," Angel replied, ending the conversation. "Matilda will be along with tea soon."

Rory wanted a stiff drink, but settled on a cup of tea like everyone else. She'd often wondered what it would be like to be home again and then she remembered why she hadn't returned in the first place.

Austin sat next to Rory, casually sipping her tea. When Mick smiled at her, she returned the gesture. *At least he seems nice. Those two look like they're itching to kill each other.* She thought, referring to Rory and her mother, who sat across from each other.

"I'm bushed from the flight. Do you mind if we continue this at dinner?" Rory was no longer in the mood to argue with her mother.

"I don't see why not. You two go get settled in."

Rory tipped her chin to Austin. They both stood and walked towards the staircase in the foyer. Halfway up, Rory turned to her. "I'm really sorry. I should've known it would be like this."

"It's not a problem, Rory. Your family seems nice."

"She's being civil because you're here. Trust me, it's not over yet and she's liable to give you the third degree before our trip is over."

"Oh," she replied, not knowing what to say. She knew nothing about Rory's family beyond the fact that they were obviously rich.

They turned down the main hallway and found their luggage outside of two rooms that were opposite each other.

"You should be pretty comfortable in there. Let me know if you need anything. Matilda is a godsend; she'll help you out with Angel if we get separated while we're here. Trust me, I don't plan to be here the entire time. I'll appease her tonight, but tomorrow we're out of here."

"Okay. I think I'll study until it's time for dinner. I

slept a lot on the plane."

"Sounds good. I need to set up my laptop and call the office. I'll do anything to keep her out of my hair."

Austin laughed. "Hey, Rory, uh…would… Do you think you could maybe show me around later?"

Rory chuckled. "It depends on how much time you have. This estate is nearly a hundred acres."

"Wow!"

"How about after dinner? I'll take you on the grand tour."

"Sounds great."

~ ~ ~

Dinner couldn't have gone by slower for Rory. She sat in ice cold silence and ate her three course meal while her mother tried desperately to talk to her. Mick did his best to intervene. Austin answered every one of the twenty questioned that Angel had asked her.

"I'm going to take Austin on a tour of the property and we'll probably been gone for a while, so I'll see you in the morning," Rory said to her mother and uncle.

"I would like to speak to you in the library before you step out, Rory," Angel replied.

Here we go. "Sure. Austin, if you will excuse me. I'll come up and get you in a few minutes." Rory followed her mother into the spacious room with floor to ceiling shelves full of books. Angel walked over to a small glass and steel cart, pouring two glasses of Brandy from the sifter. She handed one to her daughter, and then sat down across from her in one of the antique leather chairs.

"You've hardly spoken to me since you blew-in."

Angel sipped the warm liquid.

"What do you want me to say to you? Hi, how are you, how's life? I really don't care."

"Rory, I wish you weren't so hostile with me. Every time I speak to you, you're pissing vinegar."

"How would you prefer me to be?"

Angel sighed, sipping her Brandy. "I see your company is doing well."

"Did you expect it to fail?"

"I never said that. I have a prezzy for you."

"Why bother?"

"Rory Zane Eden, last Sunday was your birthday. That's a date I could never forget."

"You called, or rather had Uncle Mick call so I'd talk to you, wasn't that enough?"

"No, it's never enough. I haven't seen you in two and a half years."

"Whose fault is that?"

"You won't see me, Rory. What am I suppose to do? Then, when you finally blow-in out the blue, you have some new mate with you…"

"Don't even put her in this. She's a friend and in case you haven't noticed, I'm here on business."

"Why isn't Martie with you? I thought you two were…uh…"

"Martie is my best friend and the vice president of my company."

"Who is this girl, Austin?"

"She's…I really don't want to get into this with you. My life and my friends are none of your business."

"Here," Angel said, changing the subject and handing Rory a small box wrapped in silver and gold paper.

Rory opened the box. She was speechless as she wiped a tear from her cheek.

"It was…" Angel started to speak, fighting back her own tears.

"I know…why now…after all this time?"

"He was your daddy. No one else will ever understand the bond between you and that man and you deserve to have it. He wore that pendant around his neck until the day he died. I'd fought with his family for years to get it for you. After uh…your grandmother sent it to me after the accident and the last time you were here all we did was fight. I guess I've been waiting for the right time when I saw you again to give it to you."

Rory took the heavy, solid gold Irish Celtic Cross out of the box. It was attached to a short gold rope chain. She closed her eyes and held it tightly in her hands.

"I know now's not the time to open the wounds of the past between us, but we really do need to talk, Rory."

"We will. I need some time."

"You look just like him. It's like looking at a ghost as you get older."

"I know. I'm starting to see him in the mirror looking back at me."

~ ~ ~

Austin walked around the foyer admiring all of the artwork. She hadn't noticed the man behind her until he spoke, startling her.

"Our parent's were big art collectors. Don't let it fool you, Angel and I are true-blue under all of this."

Austin smiled at him, not understanding a word he

was saying to her.

"Come on, Angel won't let me light a lung-lolly in her house." He smiled, pulling a pack of cigarettes from his pocket.

Ah, I get it. He's going outside to smoke. Does this place come with a translator? Austin shook her head, following the man outside. He stood next to one of the large columns and lit his cigarette. "So, Rory tells me you're a surfie. Is that why she brought you?" he asked, offering her the pack.

Austin shook her head. "No thanks. I don't smoke. I do surf though. Rory's actually..." *Do I tell him she's training me? I better not start anymore drama here.* "We're friends and she invited me along to show me how things work at a pro competition."

"She's one hell of a surfie herself. Have you ever seen her in the water?"

"No, well I used to keep up with her back when she did surf. I was huge fan." *Still am.*

"She's always been a lot more than just a wax-head, but she's a bit of a bushranger around here these days."

Austin smiled. *What the hell is he saying?*

"You must be a pretty good mate for Rory to bring you into the blue between her and Angel."

"Lay off my mate, Uncle Mick. Is he being a ratbag?" Rory spoke as she walked out the front door. "I thought mum made you quit those."

"Yeah, pig's ass!" he replied.

Rory's eyes met Mick's and they both smiled. He stubbed out his cigarette and turned to go back inside. "We were just having a chin-wag. She's a ripper." He winked and smacked her arm.

"Yeah and you're a stickybeak," she called over her

180

shoulder as he walked back inside. Austin stood there staring at Rory, wondering what the hell had just happened.

"Come on. You'll get the lingo down eventually," Rory said.

They began walking towards the enormous garage on the side of the house. Rory punched in the code and the first bay opened up. A black Ford Model T Roadster was parked inside. Rory walked up to the car, opening the passenger door. She waved for Austin to get in, waiting as Austin scampered into the car. She admired the dark blue crushed velvet upholstery as Rory shut her door and walked around to the opposite side. Rory climbed in and turned the key. The old car sputtered to life.

"Rory, this is too cool!"

She met Austin's smile, shifting the car's three speed manual transmission into reverse and backing out of the garage. Then, she easily pushed in the clutch and slid it into first gear as they took off down the long driveway.

"I'm glad you like it." Rory said, driving along slowly.

"What year is it?"

"It's an original nineteen twenty six. It was my grandfather's. He gave it to me when I turned sixteen and he and I completely restored it.

"This is amazing. I love it."

The little car putted along the gravel path leading towards the back of the property.

"This is where Uncle Mick lives, up on the hill back there." Rory pointed to a large white house that was similar to the colonial style mansion that her mother lived in. She kept driving further along, coming to a smaller, more conventional looking house. "This is where Bob and Matilda live. They have a son that's a good bit younger than me, probably closer to your age. Marcus. He's away at uni I believe." Rory continued on until she crossed over another hill and drove around a bend until the path finally ended at a cliff that over looked the ocean.

"Wow. Rory, this is…it's beautiful. Did you grow up here?"

"Yeah, for the most part. This place is pretty incredible. If you take the road going in the opposite direction from the house, you'll find a nine-hole golf course," Rory said, cutting off the engine.

"Incredible is an understatement. How long has been since you've been back here?"

"Uh," Rory folded her hands on the bottom of the steering wheel. "Five years," she replied, looking away. The sun was starting to slowly drop, filling the sky with bright red and orange hues "You've never seen a real sunset, until you've seen one in Australia."

"That's for sure, it's…overwhelming," Austin murmured, glancing at the woman next to her. Rory seemed lost in thought as the sky slowly darkened.

Rory finally restarted the car and headed back down the path.

"So why haven't you been home in five years? No wonder there's so much animosity in that house."

"It's a long story."

Austin reached out, wrapping her fingers around Rory's arm before letting go. "I have all night."

"There are only a few people that know about my life, Austin. I'm not sure if I'm ready to tell another." Rory parked the small car in the same spot in the garage and turned the engine off.

When they went inside Matilda had already gone home for the day and Angel had retired to her study. "I guess I can show you around the house, and then I'm going to bed."

Austin walked next to Rory with their hands and arms touching gently here and there as they walked around the three story house. Expensive artwork was spread, with statues and paintings in every major room, including the bedrooms. Gorgeous oriental rugs covered most of the hardwood floors on the upper levels.

"This must have been an interesting place to grow up in." Austin grinned. "It really is beautiful. It's like walking around in a museum."

"Yeah. Well, I'm off to bed. I'll be across the hall if you need anything. Set your alarm so that you're up and ready for breakfast at six. After that, I want to take you somewhere, and then we'll go down to the beach."

~ ~ ~

Rory and Austin were back in the old car after having breakfast with Angel and Mick. This time, Rory had taken the opposite path from the house. Austin saw part of the golf course as they continued further on, until they came upon a cattle style fence with an open clearing with small hills, beautiful gum trees, and a tiny creek off in the distance. Rory grabbed a small bag from the car and crossed the fence. She walked out about thirty yards into the clearing and began making a strange noise.

"What the hell are you doing?" Austin asked.

"Be quiet. You'll scare him." Rory whispered back

loud enough for Austin to hear.

Scare who? Just then, a large kangaroo came hopping across the field towards Rory. *Holy shit!* The large animal stopped a few feet from Rory and she pulled a few carrots from the bag she was carrying. The reddish brown animal was nearly as tall as Rory when he stood up. He hopped closer, taking the carrots that she held out to him, before hopping off in the opposite direction.

"Did you see him?"

"Yeah!"

"Isn't he gorgeous?"

"Wow, he's fascinating."

"His name's Roo. My Grandfather got him for me when he was a Joey and we built this habitat for him. I can't believe how grown up he is."

"Can't he get out?"

"No, the fence keeps him in and he's domesticated. He has a large territory though. It's much larger than he would have had at the zoo. Uncle Mick put a female out here a few years ago, but they don't get along, so they haven't mated yet."

"That is unbelievable. You amaze me." Austin smiled as she reached out, squeezing Rory's hand. Rory froze, but she returned the warm smile before squeezing back. "There are a few koalas out there in the trees and we also have wallabies too. I forgot the binoculars, shit!"

"Don't worry about it—your kangaroo was cool enough."

"Bob is going to drop us off at the beach in a little bit. I called in some favors and I have one of my female riders bringing a stick down for you to ride. Do you think you're up to it?"

"Hell yeah!"

~ ~ ~

Rory watched as Austin paddled out behind the break. She was nervous, knowing Austin had never surfed these waters, but she'd have to get used to surfing all around the world if she wanted to join the tour.

Austin sat up on her board, watching the waves crest to six or seven foot before breaking and crashing into the shore. She'd dropped and wiped out on the first two waves. "You can do this," she said to herself. "If you choke now, this is over. You might as well kiss her goodbye."

"Come on, Austin. You can do this," Rory paced in the sand, watching Austin bob up and down on her board.

Austin took a deep breath and paddled into the line-up, backing off the first wave and dropping on the second as it crested over her head. She carved back and forth, riding the edge of her board and dragging her hand through the cool water. She rode up the face of the wave into a tight power snap off the top of the wave that let her re-enter it with more speed as she ripped back up again into a floater along the top of the wave before re-entering on last time and riding the wave until it flattened.

Austin began floating back to the beach, but stopped when she saw Rory waving.

"Get another wave!" Rory shouted, waving her arms and trying to tell Austin to stay out.

Austin shrugged, paddling back out to the line. She sat back on her board, watching each set of waves roll by. She began paddling as hard as she could, dropping on top of the next wave in the set, carving down the face to gain speed as she rode back up, launching into a front-side aerial and landing on the lip of the wave. She floated along the top of the wave before re-entering and carving down into a cutback. Then, she climbed the face of the wave, performing a snap under the lip and trimmed out the rest of the wave as it weakened.

Rory watched with a smile on her face as Austin caught another wave, and then dumped it as the water started to get choppy. She paddled back to shore.

"What did you think?" Rory asked, meeting her as Austin walked out of the water.

"It was off the hook," Austin replied with a huge grin.

Rory smiled. "Yeah, it's a lot different here than in Cali. The waves here are fast and tight," she said, handing her a dry towel. "This particular spot is tricky though. It's either going off overhead or blown out, but sometimes it closes out into the most beautiful lines you've ever seen," Rory's voice faded as her mind drifted to her past. She'd grown up surfing the very same beach.

"Did I look like a shark biscuit or whatever your uncle called me?"

Rory laughed. "No, you have the maneuvers down, Austin. There's no question about whether or not you have mad skills. You charge every wave like I've never seen, but we really need to work on flow and consistency. In a competition, power tricks are your base points so to speak and aerials are what push your score higher. We need to work on your baseline and get you doing power tricks, one right after the other, smoothly. Pumping a wave or doing cutbacks to gain speed will only hurt your score."

"Okay," Austin nodded.

"Backside surfing will get you high numbers from the start and snaps, floaters, slashes, and tail slides should be the base of your ride every time you ride a wave. Laybacks, aerials, and other extreme maneuvers, should be performed towards the end of a ride, unless it's a short line or a barrel. Then, you just have to go for whatever you can get. Also, trim the rail on long lines and inside tubes for higher points."

"I'd love to surf a tube. That would be so sweet." Austin's face lit up.

"The first time is like using your virginity. Once you do it, it's done. You can never get that first time back and it will be an experience you will never forget."

"Nice analogy...I think," she said furling her eyebrows. "My first time was horrible," Austin laughed. "Maybe my first tube wave will be a hell of a lot better!"

Rory wondered who had made her first time so unpleasant, but thinking about Austin having sex with someone else made her stomach roll. "Sophie will be here in a bit to get her board and Bob will be right behind her to take us back."

"Sophie Wood?" Austin asked.

"Yeah. She's one of my sponsored riders who lives here. She's a little taller than you, but most surfers are," Rory grinned. "I figured you'd be able to ride one her boards and I was right."

"Wow. I had no idea that's who you were talking to."

"I told you I was borrowing a board from one of my riders."

"Yeah, but I guess...hell, I don't know what I'm saying," she laughed.

~ ~ ~

Rory was still walking on eggshells around her mother when they arrived back at the house. Austin was unable to find Rory when she'd finished her shower, so she went into the lounge and opened her tablet to finish reading the last of her assigned chapters for the week.

Angel walked into the room, surprised to see the young woman alone. She jumped at the opportunity to find out why she had accompanied her daughter on the trip.

"Hi, I didn't see you there," Austin said, swallowing the lump in her throat as she smiled.

"I was actually looking for Rory."

"I haven't seen her since I got out of the shower."

Angel walked further into the room, taking the seat across from her. "So, Austin, how do you know my daughter?"

"We…uh, we met at her office."

Angel nodded. "So, you're a surfer, I presume?"

"Yes ma'am. She doesn't sponsor me or anything."

"Oh, really? Why did she bring you with her then? I guess I'm confused," she smiled slyly.

"She wanted me to see the competition."

"Bob informed me that you two went to the beach this morning."

"Yes ma'am. I went surfing and she watched."

"I see," Angel furled her brow and sipped the tea she was holding. "Do you have a boyfriend back in the states?"

"Uh…no."

"Are you a student?"

"Yes ma'am, at California State."

Angel nodded her head, pursing her lips. "What exactly are your intentions with Rory? Forgive me if I sound like a stickybeak. I guess I'm slightly confused. My daughter has only ever brought one person here. Have you met Martie?"

Austin nodded. She'd only encountered the woman once, and it hadn't been the most pleasurable experience.

"Rory and Martie have been inseparable for many years. You can see why I'm surprised that she isn't here and yet, you are."

"Ms. Zane, Rory and I are…"

"G'day, mate," Mick grinned, walking up to Austin.

"Hi." Austin smiled in relief.

"If you will excuse me," Angel said. "I need to ring my office."

Mick watched his sister walk out of the room. "Don't let her knock you. She's a polly, but really she's been a bounce since we were ankle-biters. She's spewin' with Rory for bringing you here. The barney between them has nothing to do with you. She'll be right."

Austin stared at him, wondering what the hell he was saying. "If you see Rory, let her know I went up to my room to get some work done."

"No worries."

Austin nodded and disappeared up the stairs.

~ ~ ~

Mick walked into the garage, where Rory was tinkering with her old car. He walked over to the small refrigerator next to the workbench, pulling out two beers.

"I miss seeing this thing out and about," he said,

handing Rory a beer before opening the passenger door and sitting in the seat.

"I'd love to ship it across the pond, but it'd probably cost me my inheritance to do it." Rory smiled, wiping her hand on a rag and opening the beer.

"Your mum had Austin cornered in the lounge when I walked inside," he said. "I think she's ready to give her the flick."

"Bloody hell. I knew we should've stayed in the hotel."

"You know how she is. So what's the real story?"

"Uncle Mick, it's complicated."

"It must be something since you brought her here. Your mum seems to think something happened with you and Martie."

Rory tossed the rag on top of the tool box and closed the engine panel. "Martie and I will always be best mates. Austin has nothing to do with that. "

"Well, are you having the naughty with her?"

"Uncle Mick! What the bloody hell makes you think I'm going to talk to you about my sex life?"

"I think you're cracking onto her." He laughed. "Good on ya, I say. She's a spunk."

Rory shook her head and smiled. "It's way more complicated than that and if you ever tell my mother that I'm a lesbian, I'll make sure you disappear, you ratbag."

"Rory, your mum's cunning as a dunny rat. She's known for a while now."

"What do you mean?"

"Start this old heap and let's take a drive," he said, grabbing another couple of beers from the fridge.

Rory obliged. She wasn't sure she wanted to have this conversation, but it was too late to turn back. She drove through the rolling hills, stopping alongside the cattle fence on the backside of the property.

"Roo looks good," she said. "I saw him this morning."

"Yeah, I'm beginning to think he needs a different mate."

"Maybe...Hell, I don't know."

"You think he's like you?" Mick pursed his lips.

"As in he needs a male mate?" Rory laughed, shaking her head. "I have no idea. Have you ever heard of a gay kangaroo?"

Mick laughed hysterically, shaking his head no.

"Me either. Maybe she's just not his type."

"I bought another Jill. She should be here next week, so I guess we'll see. Unless, maybe the Jill we have is the problem. Bloody hell, I may have just bought her a new mate," he said laughing again.

"Nice," she smiled, shaking her head.

"Maybe I should bring your mum out to see him. She's pretty good at reading people."

"How long has she known about me?" Rory asked, opening her second beer.

He shrugged. "Uni, I guess. I don't remember her cracking the shits about it until you were here for your first championship tour."

"Did you tell her?"

"Fuck me. You know better than that."

"Well, how did she find out then?" Rory asked, running her hand through her hair.

"A mum's instinct, I guess," he replied, watching the large kangaroo hopping in the distance. "You're her kid too. Sometimes, I think you forget that."

"Yeah, well she forgot I was someone else's kid too. I'll never forgive her, Uncle Mick."

"She knew what is was like to be a battler and she never wanted you to have that life. She made a blue, Rory."

"Yeah, well it was one big fucking mistake then."

He opened another beer and changed the subject.

"I remember the day you were here for that first competition. All eyes were on you, especially the eyes of one yank surfie that you'd brought home with you. You pretty much stood out like a shag on a rock when you walked around grinning at her like a shot fox." Mick shook his head, smiling. "Your mum nearly spit the dummy."

Rory grinned, remembering the time he was referring to. She'd just come home for the first time since leaving for college on the other side of the world and had brought her girlfriend, Martie, along with her.

"You're very lucky she never caught you two having the naughty. If Bob had nine lives, he blew right through half of them that weekend," he laughed, shaking his head.

Rory giggled. "Oh yeah, I forgot he found us in the back of the car."

Mick laughed. "The following week, he told your mum the car was shit house and got her to trade it in."

"Oh, for fuck's sake," Rory chuckled.

"Angel was mad as a cut snake, but after you won your first tour and then graduated uni; she stopped cracking the shits. Then…the accident really brought everything back that she'd gone through with your father and…it was just too much for her, Rory. I think she realized in that moment, when Martie never left your side, that she was going to have to learn to accept your

192

life and accept her in it," he shrugged. "They spent a lot of time together while you were in the hospital. Hell, we all did."

"Martie and I had broken up long before the accident. We're much better mates than anything else. Trust me. We're not each other's type at all."

"I don't think your mum knew that. She definitely wasn't very impressed when you blew in here yesterday with a schoolie that's grinning at you like a shot fox."

Rory sighed. "She's not exactly that young."

"Don't get me wrong, I like Austin. But, why did you really bring her with you?"

"She wants to join the pro tour and I've been sort of showing her the ropes."

"Are you surfing again?"

"No! Hell, no. I wanted to see how she handled competition waves and let her see how things go at a big competition."

"I think there's more to it."

Rory stared through the windshield, smiling when she saw Roo. "I care for her, Uncle Mick, but she's so young and I'm a washed up has been. She has so much ahead of her."

"So do you. Rory, you're only thirty. You still have your whole bloody life ahead of you. If this Sheila makes you happy, then give it a fair go."

Rory rubbed the gold pendant hanging on the chain around her neck. "We should probably get back. I'm sure Matilda will have dinner on the table soon."

Chapter Twelve

The next day Rory, Austin, and Mick arrived at the competition. Rory stepped out of the limo with Austin, and Mick walked around from the other side. "Your mum's gone to the office—she's buried in cat shit, so she won't be here today."

"That's fine. I wasn't expecting her anyway," Rory said, walking towards the crowded beach.

"Here come the flies," Mick exclaimed as the fans flocked towards them.

Rory smiled and shook hands with the women and men as she signed her name on calendars, pictures, magazines, t-shirts, towels, hats, surfboards and anything else they pushed into her face. Austin wasn't sure where to go, but Mick pushed her closer to Rory, nodding with a smile on his face.

After signing the last item, Rory walked towards the competitor's tent.

"I can't believe you signed that girl's bikini," Austin laughed, shaking her head.

Rory chuckled. "Yeah, I get some odd requests sometimes. I generally don't go to many of the surf competitions for a lot of reasons, this being one of them. I know I still have fans, but to me, all of this," she said, fanning her arm towards the crowded beach. "This is over for me," she sighed. "Come on, I'll introduce to the best surfers in the world."

"I'm already standing next to the best one," Austin whispered.

~ ~ ~

The competition started out casually. Many of the magazines and sportscasters took photos of Rory and spoke to her in brief interviews. She was glad to see they'd finally stopped asking when she was coming back into the sport. Austin tried to stay close by her so that she could see how everything worked behind the scenes, but she finally took a spot on the sand with the rest of the crowd as the surfers began taking to the waves. She watched the surfers in the water, studying the line-up. One wave would be perfect and a surfer would drop, having an awesome ride, then the next wave would be flat, leaving the others to wait their turn. Eventually, everyone had ridden at least one wave, completing the heats.

"What do you think?" Rory said, sitting down on the beach towel next to Austin.

"Hey. It's crazy out there. They're waiting for the perfect wave, not knowing what the next line will look like. It's completely unpredictable and nothing like what I'm use to, that's for sure."

"Yeah, it's like a game of poker. You never know what you'll be dealt, but you still have to play your hand when you're in the blind." Rory leaned closer, bumping her shoulder into Austin's. "So, you think you can do it?"

"Right now? I'd be scared to death and probably wipe out and drown," Austin replied without thinking. She turned to face the woman sitting closer to her. "I'm...so"

Rory smiled. "It takes time. No one is perfect when they first go pro."

"You were," Austin said softly, wishing she could see the pale blue eyes hidden behind Rory's dark sunglasses.

Rory laughed. "Yeah, well, I was a horse of a different color I guess," she replied, drawing in the sand with her finger.

"With consistent practice, I know I could do it, Rory. I really wish I lived somewhere like this, with real waves to surf. We have bathtub ripples at home."

"No kidding."

~ ~ ~

After the competition finals, Rory met with her riders to take pictures and congratulate them all for placing in the top three of their divisions. Austin accompanied her. She mingled with them, asking a hundred questions about the tour and riding so many different styles of waves. She was as thrilled as a child in a room full of Disney characters.

Rory saw the fire burning in her gray eyes. *She has the drive and the skill, but the heart...does she have the heart to give up everything in one ride?* Rory walked away from the crowd, sitting on a large rock, alone. She rubbed the pendant hanging just below her collarbone, while watching the waves rise and fall, one after the other, lower and lower as the tide washed away. "What the hell am I doing?" she said to herself as she wiped away a single tear.

Mick found her a few minutes later, silently sitting down next to her. Rory mustered a tiny smile.

"It's great to see you back at a pro comp, but not if it hurts you this badly," he said. "I know why you did it." He paused, watching the waves roll in. "Rory, is she worth it?"

Rory sighed. "I haven't been near the ocean for anything in over four years, except to run the beach behind my house. I stopped feeling the allure of the ocean when my ears became deaf to the call of the crashing waves. I accepted that it was over and moved on with my life." She wiped another tear from her cheek. "After all of these years, it's come back to me. That girl makes me feel again and it scares me to death. I tried so hard to ignore the magnetism pulling me towards her, but I have no control. I'm helpless against it. The walls that I carefully built around me are crashing down. She's turned my life upside down and she has no idea what she's done."

Mick wrapped his arm around her shoulders. "You either have to let her go or accept that she's freed you to live again. It's your choice." He pulled her against him. "I hate seeing you so distraught, but I also haven't seen you as happy in years as I have in the past couple of days."

Rory sighed. "I'm afraid...I feel like the closer I get to her, the closer I get to the water. If I open myself completely to her...I don't know what will happen. I swore I'd never surf again, but I'm scared to death that I may have no control over that either."

"You're only going to do what Rory wants to do deep down. Nothing and no one can make you do otherwise. Never forget that. If she's made you hear the waves again and feel the power of that call, then I think she's an angel sent from above," he said, wiping tears of his own. He'd waited so long for Rory to find her way back to the ocean and if it took the innocence of a young woman to do it, then so be it. His niece had simply become a shell of her former self and he'd give anything to have the Rory from before the accident, return.

"I definitely feel like she's something from out of this world," Rory said, taking a deep breath as she removed her sunglasses, rubbing her eyes and drying her face. She smiled at him before putting the dark glasses back on.

"Let's get out of here. We look like a pair fruitcakes," He grinned, standing up.

Rory laughed. "You're a mess, Uncle Mick."

~ ~ ~

After dinner, Rory announced that she was going for a walk. Austin decided to go with her to stretch her legs and work off the large meal she'd eaten. Mick went home for the night and Angel retired to her study to work from home, which was something she was used to doing nightly.

"Want to talk?" Austin finally asked as they followed along the path towards the cliff overlooking the ocean. She'd stayed quiet, walking casually next to Rory as the road wound through the hills.

"What's there to talk about?" Rory kicked a rock with her flip flop.

"I don't know. You looked kind of sad when we left the beach today."

"It's hard on me...the competitions and everything....I still have a really hard time going to them."

"It's been four years now, hasn't it?" Austin asked.

"Yeah, something like that," Rory replied, picking up the pace slightly.

Sensing she wasn't ready to talk about her accident, Austin changed the subject. "Tell me about your family."

"Okay, what's there to tell? They're Australian nutcases!" Rory grinned.

"Come on, Rory. How about your father?"

Rory gazed up at the orange sky. *Where to start. Should I even tell her?* "My dad was the apple of his family's eye. Randall Eden was one hundred percent Irish, born and raised in Dublin, Ireland, despite having blond hair and blue eyes. I actually look a lot like him. Anyway, he'd gone on vacation in California in the summer before his senior year of college. He'd been studying to be a businessman like his father. They owned a few bed and breakfasts in the countryside." She paused, touching the gold pendant and smiling as she thought about her father.

"Angel grew up here at the Zane Estate. Her grandparents were rich in mineral mining, but her father left the family business after only a few years, choosing to spend his early life as an attorney with his own law practice before moving into politics, having become the attorney-general and minister for justice of Queensland at one point. Her mother was a philanthropist, serving on multiple committees. Angel wanted to follow in her father's footsteps and had been about to start her third year of uni after being accepted to law school early. She flew to California to celebrate and met my father one afternoon on the beach."

Rory looked out at the miles of ocean as they neared the end of the path.

"They fell madly in love, spending every minute together. My mother found out she was pregnant a week before she had been scheduled to fly home. When she told my father, he asked her to marry him. He didn't want to go to Australia and she didn't want go to Ireland, so they were married at the justice of the peace and settled down outside of Long Beach. They'd gone against the wishes of both of their families and in doing so, were disowned. I was born the following March and—"

Austin grabbed Rory's arm. "You mean to tell me you had a birthday this month and you didn't say anything? That's rude."

"How is it rude?" Rory grinned.

"Well, what if I wanted to get you something?"

"You're too late…it was….last Sunday."

"Happy Birthday. I can't believe you didn't tell me. So how old…wait you'd be about twenty nine, am I right?"

"Thirty."

"Wow."

"I know. I told you I'm a washed up old sock." Rory smiled.

"No you're not."

"Well, I'm definitely a lot older than you are."

"It's only a number. Age doesn't define someone," Austin said.

"True, you're still so damn young though. When I

was your age I didn't have a care in the world."

"Enough about me and my age, get back to your story," Austin growled.

"Well, as I said, I was born in March, but before that, my father had decided to change his major and become an architect because he loved to design things. He received an engineering degree a year later. My mother finished her degree and started taking law classes on the side and working for a small law firm. They barely had anything after being dumped by their families, but they'd had each other and to them, that was all that they'd needed.

Anyway, my father is the one who taught me how to surf. He had learned the summer that he and my mother met. He started taking me surfing when I was three and continued on until..." Rory stopped next to the railing. She looked down at the waves crashing against the jagged rocks below.

Austin felt the change in the woman next to her and looked up to see tears in her eyes.

"My father became very ill all of a sudden when I was seven. He died of cancer three months later, he was only thirty." She took a deep breath, wiping the tears from her eyes.

"Angel packed everything up and pulled me out of school. Three weeks after his funeral, we moved back here to the family estate on the Gold Coast. She went back to her maiden name and pushed my father completely out of her life. Her family accepted me with open arms, but it took a lot for her to work her way back in. She went to law school full time. Uncle Mick had already finished law school and had his own firm. He and his wife Lucy practically raised me because Angel was too caught up in school for anything else and honestly, I was a daily reminder of the best time of her life and the biggest mistake she'd ever made," Rory tossed a small rock over the cliff, losing sight of it as it descended.

"She graduated and became my uncle's law partner, until my grandfather helped her move into politics. After I graduated high school, I moved to La Jolla and never looked back. From the time I was seven until I turned eighteen my mother never spoke of my father. My father's family went nuts when she informed them that he'd been cremated. That had been his last wish. He wanted to be spread in the ocean and my mother did what he wanted. They tried to come after her, but had no legal leg to stand on. It was a huge mess and because of that, she forbade me to ever have anything to do with them."

"Oh my God, that's terrible." Austin grabbed Rory's hand.

"Yeah, the only thing I had to keep me going through my childhood was surfing, and of course, Uncle Mick. He wasn't very good at it, but he went surfing with me every single day. His wife left him for some bloke in Melbourne when I was a teenager. He was pretty heartbroken, but it just brought him and me closer. The older I got, the worse things became between my mother and me. She found out I had contacted my paternal grandparents right before I graduated high school and literally flipped out on me. That was the icing on the cake. I never felt at home here. It sounds stupid I guess, but California will always be my home. To me, that's where my dad is."

"That makes sense," Austin said.

"After my first year, she tried to come see me, but I

was busy with school and I had been picked up by a few sponsors, so I began surfing the pro tour. I managed to graduate with a double major before winning my second championship. I also worked part time as a design engineer for the board company that sponsored me. I guess you know as well as the rest of the world, I was on my way to winning my fourth championship...that's when..." Rory drew in a deep breath and whispered. "That's when my world ended."

"I'm so sorry, Rory." Austin let go of her hand to wipe away her own tears. She couldn't imagine going through the life Rory had just described. It made her want to go see her mother now more than ever. She hated living on the opposite side of the country, but her mother understood she was following her dreams.

"Angel was running for Queensland State Senator when I had the accident. She came to the hospital, but then she tried to bring me back here to recover and do my physical therapy. I refused. She left and ironically six months later she was elected. I saw her once after that a couple of years ago when she showed up at one of the pro surfing events here because she read in a magazine that I'd be there. We had a huge argument and I haven't seen her since."

"Wow. Did she use your accident to get voted into office?"

"I'm pretty sure she won the sympathy vote whether she wanted to or not. It was national news, but I really don't care. She's always done what she wanted to do and the hell with everyone else. I learned a long a time ago that it's Angel Zane's way, or no way."

"Do you at least talk on the phone with her?" Austin

questioned.

"She calls me, or tries to anyway. I never talk to her. She relies on Martie to keep her updated on my life."

"Oh...that must be the hot-tempered woman I've seen you with."

Rory laughed. "Yeah, that's Martie, uh...Martina Cruz, she's the Vice President of my company, along with many, many other titles."

"I see." *I hope lover isn't one of them.* "You're mom asked me about her or rather wanted to know why I was here with you and she wasn't."

"I'm not surprised. Uncle Mick and I had an interesting conversation about my mum earlier."

"Was he asking the same thing?"

"No, he knows why you're here."

"Why is that? I mean I know you wanted me to surf bigger sets and see the competition, but why am I really here, Rory?"

Rory chucked another rock over the rail. "Crashing waves," she murmured.

"Huh?"

Rory sighed. "I...I uh...I lost everything in that accident. During my recovery I realized my ears were deaf to the call of the ocean and I'd lost my passion for surfing. I had no desire to go near the water ever again. Everything inside of me died that day." Rory wiped away a tear as she turned to face the woman next to her. "I can't explain it and I don't know how you did it, but Austin, you made me hear the waves and feel the power of the ocean's magnetism again." Rory stepped closer. "This connection between us scares the hell out of me," she whispered just before her lips touched Austin's, ending the internal tango that her heart and mind had been dancing together for the past three months.

The kiss was gentle and slightly hesitant as Rory's heart beat wildly in her chest. She felt Austin's lips part, beckoning her inside. Rory wrapped her arms around Austin's waist, pulling her closer as she deepened the kiss, tasting the woman that had brought her back to life. Austin threaded her arms around Rory's neck, pressing her body fully against Rory's as she returned the kiss intensely, feeding the craving that had been eating away at her since the night they'd shared the tentative, New Year's kiss on the beach.

Rory pulled away breathlessly, staring at the unmasked gray eyes gazing back at her. The desire she saw in them frightened her and fueled the fire burning in her belly at the same time. The cool breeze swirling between them felt like needles on her skin in every place that her body had been heated by Austin's. Rory reached up, running her fingers softly over Austin's cheek. Austin turned into the touch, closing her eyes as Rory's fingers grazed her heated lips. Rory bit her bottom lip, sighing as the last of the breath that she'd been holding, escaped her lungs.

Austin turned ravenous eyes on her once more. Rory had never felt anything like the raw hunger that was driving her. She struggled to breathe, swallowing the lump in her throat. She no longer had control of her body or her mind. The unbridled lust burning deep inside her was like drowning all over again. It scared her to death.

"We can't do this," Rory finally whispered.

Austin put her hand on Rory's chest slightly below her collarbone to steady herself. She was lightheaded from the arousal racing through her veins. Their heated kiss had only scratched the surface and her body yearned for more.

"What?" Austin gasped.

Rory put her hands on Austin's waist to steady her. "Whatever this is between us…it's…it's too much. I can't do this." Rory stepped away and began walking back down the moonlit path.

It took Austin a second to digest what she'd said.

"That's insane," Austin huffed, catching up to her. "You want me just as badly as I want you. Damn it, you can't deny it!" she grabbed Rory's arm as she slowed to a stop. "I felt it. Rory, I felt *you.*"

Rory spun around into her, pushing Austin back against a large gum tree near the side of the gravel path. She pressed her body against Austin's, holding her in place and kissing her hard. Austin put her hands in Rory's hair, tugging and returning the kiss as if Rory was the air her body needed to survive. Rory rocked into her, biting Austin's bottom lip as the flames of desire smoldered inside of her, taking over. She moved her hand from Austin's side to the waistband of her shorts, slipping easily under it.

Austin's breath hitched and her heart raced as she felt Rory's fingers skim across the flesh between her legs. All rational thought had left her erotically intoxicated brain long ago. She was nearly in agony, aching deep inside with anticipation.

Rory pulled Austin's soaked panties to the side, sliding her fingers through the wetness and easily inside of her, pushing her fingers deeper as she kissed her harder. The hunger coursing through Rory veins was driving her wild. She felt alive.

Austin pulled out of the kiss, gasping for air and

grinding herself between the tree and Rory's body as Rory's fingers drove in and out of her. Hot wetness covered the palm of Rory's hand as she pressed it against Austin's throbbing center. Austin tugged hard on the short hair at the back of Rory's head as Rory kissed her hard once more, nearly drawing blood as she bit her lower lip.

A guttural moan escaped Austin's mouth as she panted heavily, breathing like a caged bull. Beads of sweat ran from her forehead down the sides of her face. The boiling blood surging through her body roared loudly in her ears. Rory pushed another finger inside of her and Austin screamed out, thrusting down as hard as she could as the orgasm tore through her body, rendering her senseless. She collapsed against the woman holding her up.

The feral appetite driving Rory's wild nature dissipated as she slowly caught her breath. She pulled her hand free, backing away from Austin. Her nerves stung as the air cooled her heated body. It had been so long since she'd last touched another woman and the feverish magnetism between them had nearly driven her mad with urgency.

"I'm so sorry," Rory whispered.

Austin wiped her face on the sleeve of her t-shirt as the blood moved slowly back down to her wobbly legs. Her ragged breathing was starting to calm. "Sorry for what?" she replied.

"That was completely barbaric of me. I...I don't know what came over me." *Oh my God, what have I done?* Rory ran her hand through her hair. "Did I hurt you?"

"Hey," Austin stepped closer, running her hand over

Rory's cheek and meeting her eyes. "You definitely did not hurt me, Rory. You took me by surprise, but I never wanted you to stop."

Rory tried to comprehend what had transpired between them and justify her actions, but the uncontrolled passion terrified her. "I've never been aggressive like that with anything, except surfing, and surely never another person. That will never happen again."

"I hope you're not serious," Austin chided.

"I'm very serious. It was unintentional and I apologize," Rory said as she turned around and walked away. *I completely lost control of myself.*

~ ~ ~

As soon as the sun rose the next morning, Angel met her daughter as she descended the staircase, asking her to step into the library. Rory sighed and followed her down the hall. She wasn't in the mood for another go around with her mother. All she wanted to do was get on a plane and fly as far away from Australia as fast as possible, but the thought of sitting next to Austin for the eighteen hour journey made her queasy.

"Have a seat," Angel said, sitting across from her.

Here we go...again. Rory sighed. "We don't have to do this now."

"Yes. Yes, we do."

"Fine."

"Rory, for what it's worth...I'm sorry," she ended just above a whisper.

"Don't do this now, you're too late..."

"I know...I...ever since your accident..."

208

"Please..."

"I almost lost you too...Rory,"

Rory saw the tears running down her mother's face and felt a tear of her own slip away. "I can't just forget..."

"I don't expect you to. I know I was wrong..."

"Wrong? You kept me from my family and you took him from me!" Rory yelled.

"I didn't know what else to do..."

"It's not that easy. I'll never forgive you. You tossed me aside and forced me to believe my grandparents were the reason you kept me from my father's family. He was my God damn father!"

"I know Rory, I know and I'm so sorry. I can't apologize enough for the things I did when you were younger. I did what I thought was best for both of us."

"That's bullshit and it's way too late for sorry. You pretty much wrote me off too, when I moved away from here. At least until my accident, which by the way you obviously used to get yourself elected so way to go. I'm glad I was able to help you out by cracking my skull and drowning! I fucking died on that beach and you didn't give a shit," Rory screamed as tears poured down her cheeks.

"That's not true. I rushed to your side. You're my daughter, Rory, and no matter how much you hate me or think that I hate you, I will always love you."

"Then why the fuck did you leave me in that hospital when I refused to come back here to recover? I couldn't walk, I couldn't talk, I barely knew who the fuck I was and you just left me! I hated you for making me feel like I wasn't worth your time!"

Angel stared at the floor, wiping tears from her face.

"You…you needed Martie more than you needed me. She was the one you were asking for and wanting to see when you finally woke up from the coma. What was I supposed to do? I can't compete with her. I never could. She replaced me in your life a long time ago and I've learned to accept that."

"Martie? She has nothing to do with this. You're my fucking mother!" Rory shook her head. "I get it now. You'd taken everything else from me and tried to take her away by bringing me here to recover, but it didn't work. She was the one thing you were unable to take away. When are you going to wake up and accept that I'm an adult and you can't run my life?"

"Rory, you pushed me completely out of your life when you moved away. Then, you brought Martie with you the first time you came back and I thought you were making the same mistakes I had made. I didn't want you to suffer the heartache that I had gone through. Your father and I were barely making ends meet before he became sick."

"Yeah, but no matter what, you were both happy."

"That's true, we were about as happy as anyone could be living in a shack and barely making enough money to pay the bills."

"That's not my life."

"I know. I realized after your accident, that you had everything you'd ever wanted in your life. You'd found happiness and become very successful all on your own. I was so proud of you and I didn't know how to tell you that and it was too late. Your world had shattered in an instant, just like mine, but the difference was, you had Martie there to pick up the pieces."

"You left because you thought I'd replaced you in my

life with Martie? That's ridiculous. You're my mother. She's my best friend."

"We both know she's more than that and...I'm glad you have her in your life."

"She'll always be there, but only as my best friend," Rory corrected.

"Is that because of the schoolie you brought with you?"

"Austin is just a friend. She has nothing to do with any of this. Martie and I had broken up long before the accident because we're better off as friends. If you'd been an actual mother to me all of these years, you would've known that."

"Fine. There's no need to continue beating a dead horse, Rory."

"I need to get ready to go. The last thing I want to do is miss my flight," Rory said, walking out of the room.

Angel saw Austin coming down the stairs with her suitcase a few minutes later. "Bob would've brought that down for you."

"Thank you, but I've got it."

Angel stepped closer. "I don't know you and I don't know what your intentions are with my daughter, but Rory's an extraordinary person and if she allows you in her life, you must be pretty exceptional yourself. Trust me. I know what it's like firsthand to be on the outside looking in. If you care for her, like I believe you do, hold on tight and never let go."

Chapter Thirteen

Rory had been back from Australia for nearly three weeks. Despite how hard she tried, she couldn't get Austin off her mind. She avoided her on the long flight home and had gone as far as blocking all of her calls. She was scared she'd be tempted to go into the fire smoldering between them again. The flames had burned her once, creating wounds that would probably never heel. She'd lost all self control, allowing the hunger deep inside of her to take over. The only time she'd ever felt like that had been when she was dropping on a double overhead wave. She'd had to let go in order to own the wave, using everything it gave her and riding it like its purpose in the ocean was solely for her use. Treating Austin aggressively and using her like the face of a wave had broken Rory, splitting her at her core.

It was too late to take it all back. The damage had been done. Feeling the same powerful yearning for Austin that she'd once felt for surfing both alarmed and terrified her. She felt paralyzed. She heard the crashing waves again and sensed the calling, but it wasn't the ocean summoning her. It was Austin.

Why do I need you so much? Rory thought of Austin as she stared at the waves washing ashore under the moonlight. She'd been sitting on the beach behind her house for the past two hours, trying to justify her actions over the last few months. She had been driven by a passion that ran through her like the blood in her veins. Nothing made sense, yet everything circled back around to the young woman who had invaded her mind and her heart.

Regardless of how badly she wanted to turn away from Austin and run in the opposite direction, Rory knew the fighting was over. She was defeated. She'd finally come to terms with knowing that Austin had come into her life for a reason. Austin awakened parts of her that she thought were dead and gone, making her feel alive again. Her soul had risen from the bottom of the ocean floor. Denying it, she would only be lying to herself.

~ ~ ~

Rory had made a promise to Austin and she intended to keep it. The next morning, she dressed in black pants with a light blue blouse that brought out her baby blue eyes, and drove towards the address on the invitation that she'd received two days before.

She arrived at the concert style arena with twenty minutes to spare as she parked in an open space and walked inside. Thousands of friends and family members were seated in the upper and lower level areas and the arena floor was full of graduates sitting in folding chairs.

Rory took a seat on the side in the lower level, but was still too far away to make out any of the students' faces.

~ ~ ~

The commencement ceremony had finally begun. Austin was tired from spending the last two days with her mother and father since they'd arrived separately. She wished they'd just get along enough to see her graduate and then go back to their separate lives. She stared up at all of the people in the surrounding seats, wondering where each of them had decided to sit. Her chest ached, knowing the one person that she had wanted to be there more than anything, wasn't. She hadn't heard from Rory since the day they'd said goodbye in the airport. Austin wasn't sure who was happier, Rory or Lori, when she saw that Lori had surprised her, arriving in time to pick her up. She'd left half a dozen messages and had sent her an invitation to the ceremony. All had gone unanswered.

Austin wasn't exactly sure where things had gone wrong in Australia. One minute, she was asking Rory about her family and the next, she was up against a tree with the world spinning off its axis around her. Seeing the raw desire in Rory's eyes and feeling it as she touched her, had been the most incredible experience of her life. She craved Rory like a desert awaiting a thunderstorm. It scared and excited her. Knowing she may never see Rory again, made her feel frozen and numb. She'd been going through the motions for the past few weeks, finishing her final exams, and making sure she had everything in line to graduate, all while working double shifts and surfing every day. She was tired, but sleep had been the farthest thing from her mind each night.

~ ~ ~

Rory watched as the two hour ceremony finally ended. Each graduate stood, tossing their cap into the air and cheering. She smiled, remembering what that day had been like for her. Her mind drifted back to Angel and the heated conversation they'd had just before she'd left, but her eyes locked onto Austin before her thoughts could go any further. She quickly made her way through the crowd, stopping when she noticed Lori and an older woman with blond hair who was rushing up to Austin with her arms spread wide. She watched the mother and daughter exchanging hugs and wiping away tears as they smiled together. She thought of Angel again and the relationship she longed for, but would never have. A man with brown hair and a thin beard walked up to the group, hugging Austin. When she saw Lori wrap her arms around Austin's neck, she turned to walk away.

"Rory?" Austin questioned, staring at the impeccably dressed woman. She grabbed her arm, spinning her around.

"Congratulations," Rory said. "I…uh…I should go."

"No, please don't go." Austin reached out, interlacing her fingers with Rory's and pulling her along. "These are my parents, Janice and Derrick."

Rory stuck her hand out, smiling briefly at Lori, who was standing between the man and woman. "Rory Eden," she said.

Janice eyed her suspiciously. Rory watched her eyes, letting go when they landed on her and Austin's joined hands.

215

"I need to get to the office, but I wanted to say congratulations."

Austin walked a few feet away from her family with Rory. "I'm glad you came...I..."

"We need to talk, but that can wait. Today is your big day. Go celebrate with your family and call me in a day or two." Rory patted her arm and walked away.

~ ~ ~

Rory walked from her office into the conference room down the hall. She opened the file she'd been carrying, displaying its contents on the table in front of her.

"I'm glad everyone was able to make this meeting on short notice. I've been going over our P&L statements for each department. We obviously know the prime of snow season has passed and we're coming up on the backbone of surf season. I wanted to let you know that we finished the snow season with record numbers. Our winter apparel line has taken off. We surpassed our budget and there are still a few months left for that category. We took on a fairly new department and a brand new category this year for snow and they have both produced unbelievable numbers. At the rate we're growing in this department, we could easily surpass Burton to be the leader in the snowboarding industry by this time next year." She paused, changing the page in front of her to another spreadsheet.

"With surf season coming to a head, we have a lot of work to do. This is our bread and butter, ladies and gentlemen. This is where we shine. We are the leader in the surfing industry and I intend to keep it that way. For the past two years, the surfing industry has driven this company and I expect this season to greatly exceed the budgeted numbers. We also have the new additions to the summer apparel line that are starting to pick up dramatically. I expect this category to exceed its budget as well. Does anyone have anything to add on the categories or departments?"

Martie spoke first. "I think the numbers that we're producing are amazing so far and if the surf department continues in the same direction that it's heading in, then we should definitely exceed all of our expectations."

"I agree, the sky is the limit," Lisa chimed in.

"Wonderful, Lisa, you'll need to make sure the April events are covered by all of our reps. I will not be attending any of the tour events for the next two months. I will however, be in France for the Roxy Jam at the end of May. I have some personal business to attend to and I'll be out of the office for about three or four weeks. I'll have my phone and laptop with me and I'll be checking in daily. Please rely on Martie with any pending or time sensitive issues. I know this isn't the best time of year for me to take some time off, but I'm confident that everyone knows how to do their jobs. Starting with the Roxy Jam, I plan to be at the rest of the events this year. Are there any questions?" She paused. "None? Wow, speechless, I love it," she said, grinning as she closed the file and stood up.

Outside of the room Martie caught up to Rory. "Don't start. Meet me in my office." Rory cut her off before she could say anything.

A few minutes later, Martie slammed the door to Rory's office. "What the hell is going on?"

"You're making an ass out of yourself. Calm down."

"Rory, I don't get you? Where are you going now?"

"I'm going back to Oahu for a little while."

"Your beach house in Pupukea? Why? You haven't been back to Hawaii since the...oh, Rory, are you sure about this?"

"Yeah, I need to go back. It's time."

"Do you want me to go with you?"

"No. You're needed here...besides—"

"You're taking her? You've barely spoken to me about your trip to Australia and you haven't mentioned her once. What happened while you were there?"

"Martie, she needs consistent training on unpredictable waves if she plans to go pro. You know how that works. Hell, that's why I bought that house anyway, for my own training."

"I can't believe you're doing this, Rory."

"It's not your—"

"Are you surfing again?" Martie wanted to choke the life out of her best friend.

Rory looked deep into Martie's green eyes. "Martina, I'm going to forget you had to even ask me that."

"I'm sorry," Martie sighed.

"Let it go. I made a promise to Austin and I'm going to follow through. I'm giving myself a few weeks to teach her how to make her style consistent and competition worthy. There's a small amateur competition at Chun's Reef, in three weeks. If she's good enough to enter that, then I'll let her. Whatever happens there will be the clincher. She'll either do really well and be able to enter the next Pro Am qualifier, or she'll fall back on the college degree she just earned. I guess we'll see."

"So you have this all worked out do you?"

"Martie, you're my best mate, back me up just this

once, please. Bloody hell, you're as cross as a frog in a sock!"

"English, Rory!" Martie shook her head.

"Oh, piss off," Rory grinned.

Martie laughed. "Alright. You want to do this, then fine, but don't say I didn't tell you otherwise. I'm not...I can't be there to pick up the pieces of your life this time, Rory. I just can't do it."

"I know. I'm not asking you to and my life's not falling apart. My company is on top and my life is finally going in some kind of direction. There's nothing you need to worry about."

"Going back to Hawaii for the first time since the accident is going to be the hardest thing you will ever do. I...I wish I was going with you."

"I know, mate. I'll be okay."

"I can't believe you're taking her there with you. There's something going on that you're not telling me."

"I can't explain it, Martie. I feel like I can give something back to the sport if what I see in her is real. It scares me to death. I don't want her to get hurt. I couldn't...I don't know what I'd do, but I made her a promise and I don't break promises."

"That's definitely the truth. Why does it have to be *her*? That's what doesn't make sense to me."

"I don't even understand it myself. She...there's something about her. She makes me enjoy surfing again. I don't know what that means."

"Are you in love with her?" Martie asked.

Rory looked across her desk and into her best friend's golden eyes. "I don't know," she sighed. "You're the only person I've ever loved, but this...this is something completely different."

"If she breaks your heart I'll beat her to death with a surfboard," Martie said, seriously.

Rory raised her eyebrows, believing without a doubt that the woman sitting across from her wasn't lying.

"When are you leaving?" Martie asked.

"As soon as I tell her and…"

"What! You haven't even talked to her about this?"

"No." Rory looked away shyly.

"You always do everything ass backwards."

"Yeah. Yeah. She's busy with her family. She graduated from Cal State yesterday."

~ ~ ~

Rory sat in the sand behind her house, nursing a glass of whiskey as she listened to the crashing waves. "I hope you know what you're doing, Eden. This could seriously backfire in your face." Rory reached up, running her fingers over the pendant that rested in the hollow of her neck. *I miss you, Dad. I know you're watching over me. I know you're the one who saved me. I'll never tell anyone, but I saw your face as you pulled me off the bottom. That's why they found me. They thought I'd started floating up after hitting my head, but you were pulling me to the surface for them to reach me.* Rory chased away the few tears they fell from her icy blue eyes and walked into the house.

Grabbing her phone from the kitchen counter, Rory scrolled through her contacts, rubbing her finger over the one she wanted to call.

"Austin?" Rory asked.

"No, this is Lori. She's in the shower—wait, here she

comes."

"Hello?" Austin answered, shaking her wet hair out.

"Hey."

"Rory, hi, what's up?"

"Uh...do you...can you meet me for dinner at the pier?"

"Hmm...I....well..." Austin shrugged her shoulders to her friend. "Sure. I'll be there in thirty minutes."

"If your family is still here, we can meet another night."

"No, they left this morning. I'll see you in a bit." Austin said before ending the call.

"You jump pretty fucking high every time she says your name."

"Damn it, Lori. This is good news. At least I hope it is."

"You're in love with her and she's going to break your heart," Lori replied, shaking her head. "I saw how hurt you looked when you came home from traveling halfway around the world with her. I wasn't the only one who saw how much you lit up when she appeared at your graduation. Your mom was staring at her like a pedophile."

"Oh good God, we're only nine years apart. I don't need this from you right now. My mom knows I'm a lesbian. She knew when I was ten," Austin growled, storming out of the room.

~ ~ ~

Dinner came and went. Rory contemplated ordering a stiff drink, but decided she had better do this

221

completely sober. "So how's school going?"

Austin laughed.

"What?" Rory raised an eyebrow.

"You were at my graduation a couple of days ago."

"Oh, right. I know that." *Great.* Rory wasn't sure how to talk to Austin. The atmosphere between them had shifted uncomfortably since their last night in Australia.

"Rory, what's wrong?" Austin asked.

"Nothing, I'm sorry. I meant how's work."

"Work is fine. The big question is, are we? I haven't heard from you since we got back."

Rory sipped her water, wishing it was stronger. "I've been busy. I know that's no excuse—"

"I overheard the conversation between you and your mother. I hadn't meant to. I was actually looking for you when I heard you both yelling."

"I guess you know why things are so bitter between us then," Rory exclaimed.

"Are you and Martie involved?" Austin questioned.

Rory met her eyes. "No. We were at one time though. We will always care for each other, but we realized a long time ago that we're better off as friends."

"Your mother seems to prefer her."

"What do you mean?"

"She grilled me while we were there. She wanted to know if I knew Martie and why was I there with you and not her. Then, after what I heard you two saying…the questioning made sense."

Rory shook her head. "She was under the impression that Martie and I were still together. I guess that's what happens when you don't talk for a number of years. There hasn't been anyone in my life for about five years…well, no one until you."

"Is that what you want? For me to be in your life?"

"I honestly don't know, Austin. I made you a promise to work with you and get you ready for the tour, but as far as anything else...I...I just don't know." Rory stared out the window at darkness. "I'm sorry if I led you to believe otherwise. What happened with us...that's..."

"If you apologize one more time for touching me, I'm going to toss this glass of water in your face. Rory, you didn't hurt me and you didn't do anything I didn't want you to do. We were caught up in a magical moment. I only regret not being able to touch you too."

Rory turned back towards her, meeting Austin's gray eyes. "If you could go anywhere in the world...where would you go?"

"Uh...okay." Austin wasn't expecting the sudden subject change. She stared at Rory for a minute, trying to read the enigmatic woman. Finally, she answered. "If I could go anywhere it would have to be Pipeline. Isn't that every surfer's dream?" Austin smiled. She watched Rory's eyes slowly close as she hung her head slightly. Austin had forgotten that was where Rory's accident had been. "Rory, I'm sor—"

Rory interrupted her, ignoring the pain she felt at the mention of the one place she never wanted to see again."How would you like to go to the North Shore for a couple of weeks?"

"What?"

"I own a beach house in Pupukea, on the North Shore of Oahu. Backdoor and Pipeline are about a mile away. The break behind my house is actually referred to as Log Cabins or Logs to the locals. It's a little smaller and easier to ride and a hell of a lot less crowded."

"No way!"

"Yeah, I bought the house after my first year on the tour. I used to live and train there pretty much year round...until my...until I stopped surfing."

"Wow..."

"Would you like to go there with me and hone your skills on real waves?"

"Of course I want to go, but are you sure?"

"Yes. I wouldn't have asked if I wasn't. When do you think you will be able to leave?"

"Tomorrow!" Austin nearly shouted.

Rory smiled. "I don't know if my secretary can get us a flight that quickly. It may be a few days. Make sure you clear it with your job. That needs to come first."

Rory paid the tab and they walked out of the restaurant together. As soon as she was in her truck, Austin scrolled through the contacts on her phone, highlighting the person she wanted to call.

"Lori you will never believe this, where are you?" she shrieked.

Chapter Fourteen

The plane landed smoothly at the Honolulu International Airport after a nearly six hour non-stop flight. The temperature was warm, in the low eighties, the sun was shining and there wasn't a cloud in the sky. Rory's chest tightened immediately when she smelled the air outside. *You can do this. Stay strong.*

"It's so beautiful here," Austin said, taking in the sights as Rory drove their rented convertible across the island.

An hour later, they pulled into the slender driveway of a small white bungalow with a small carport. The place definitely looked like a beach house. Large sand dunes and overgrown sand weeds were visible behind it and the little bit of grass in the thin strip of front yard had been mowed recently.

They grabbed their bags and Rory opened the front door. She nodded for Austin to walk in first, setting her suitcase down on the light colored bamboo floor that ran throughout the house. Austin walked further inside. A crème colored couch with light yellow and baby blue throw pillows sat against one of the bright white walls. Various beach scene paintings in light pink and baby blue frames hung on the other walls. Every part of the house was decorated with beach décor and pastel colors. A large area rug was spread over the floor under the light colored wooden coffee table in front of the couch and the hallway had a runner down the center. The opposite wall from the couch had a small entertainment center with a TV in the middle.

"My room's at the end of the hall and the first door on the left is the spare bedroom. I know it's a little small and drastically different compared to my house in Long Beach. Hell, it would probably fit in the living room of the Zane Estate with room to walk around it."

Austin laughed. "It's adorable, Rory. Quiet and quaint, I love it." She smiled.

"Across the hall from your room is your bathroom and then there is also one in the master bedroom."

Austin nodded, placing her suitcase in her room and then she walked through the French doors, leading to the small patio off the back of the house. There was a small patch of grass with a stone walkway past the patio and then nothing but large tan colored sand dunes and the sound of the ocean beyond them.

"Hey, I need to go to the grocery store and stock up the fridge and the cabinets. Do you want to stay here and unpack or go with me?" Rory called through the doorway.

"I'll go with you, that way I can help you pay for everything."

"Austin, have I ever made you pay for anything when you're with me?"

"No and I don't understand why not."

"Because you're my guest and guests don't pay for anything. Come on."

~ ~ ~

They deposited the vast amount of grocery bags on the island in the kitchen.

"I think we bought enough to feed an army," Austin laughed.

"Well, I hate to go to the store. Besides, we don't have time to shop or go to restaurants. Here, help me get these put away so I can make dinner. I'm starving."

"What are you making, Martha Stewart?" Austin teased.

"Watch it, ankle-biter!" Rory chided, turning to put away the pasta and sauce that she'd been holding, into the cabinet.

"Who are you calling ankle-biter? You ratbag!"

"Hey!" Rory spun around, facing her with a raise eyebrow at the mild insult.

"You know I'm only having a lend of you, you old bastard!" Austin grinned.

Rory raised an eyebrow, shaking her head in disbelief. "You spent too much time with Uncle Mick. You're starting to sound like that silly old codger."

Austin laughed. "Yeah, he was definitely interesting. I still don't understand half the shit he said to me."

"I don't either and I lived with the man for eleven years!" Rory laughed. "He says hello by the way and I've been told not to come back to Oz, unless I have you with me."

~ ~ ~

The Italian dinner that Rory made had been eaten in a quarter of the time that it had taken to make. The bottle of Pinot sitting on the table was still half full. Rory and Austin sat on the small couch watching reruns on the TV.

"I'm tired, so if you don't mind, I'm going to head off to bed. You can stay up if you want, but you need to be up with me at five."

"Five! Are you kidding?!"

"No. I'm going to train you the way I trained myself. We start tomorrow...at five." Rory said, spinning on her heels before walking down the hall.

"Great, some vacation this is going to be," Austin muttered to herself as she turned the TV off.

~ ~ ~

At a quarter after five, Rory was standing in the sand next to the large dunes. She was barefooted and wearing only a sports bra and shorts. Austin stood next to her, still half asleep and trying not to stare at the vast amount of tan skin that Rory was showing.

"Have you ever heard of Tai Chi?" Rory asked.

"Who?"

"Tai Chi. It's a meditation art form. I'm going to show it to you. I have been doing this everyday for about eight or nine years now."

"Okay, what do we do?"

"First we stretch."

Both women began slowly stretching their frames,

careful not to pull too hard in any one direction.

"You simply follow these basic steps..." She counted them off as she showed Austin the movements. "Then you add more to it as you get more advanced. Think you got it?"

"Maybe."

Rory began slowly moving through the steps, stretching her arms and legs and fluidly moving into different stances with Austin mimicking her every move until she had it down. Then, Rory began showing her more advanced movements. Two hours later, they were glistening with sweat and completely focused.

"That's really incredible. I've never done anything like that." Austin gulped her bottled water.

"We will wake up and do this every morning. It'll help you maintain stability and endurance, on top of keeping your mind focused. I sometimes do it at night too when I don't feel like running three or four miles, but I don't want you to get tired. You need to build up your energy. Go change and meet me back here. Make sure you're wearing a rash guard. The water's warm, so swimsuit bottoms or board shorts will be fine."

Austin disappeared into the house and Rory walked out to the shed. She had four short boards hanging on the wall. *Hmm...*She examined the boards until she was satisfied with one. Rory grabbed a block of wax, and a wash comb, before closing the door and walking back towards the beach. She frantically dropped the board that was under her arm when she realized she had been carrying it, along with the rest of the contents in her other hand.

She suddenly felt clammy as sweat began beading up

on her skin. The salt air burned her nostrils as she inhaled and her vision swam. She forced her eyes closed, willing the vomit to stay down. *No! No, please, no. Not now!* Her body convulsed and she doubled over in the grass next to the shed. Bile rose in her throat and she vomited. Tears streamed down her face when her body finally stopped dry heaving.

She quickly wiped her faced with the back of her hands as she stood up. "Yuck!" The taste in her mouth was disgusting. She spit a few times and kicked some sand over the spot in the grass. *Come on, Rory. You can do this. It's not like you're the one getting in the water. Be strong! She needs you.*

Before Rory could pick the board back up, Austin appeared.

"Is everything okay?"

"Yeah, here, go wax this up and I'll meet you in the sand. I need to run inside for a second."

Austin picked everything up and Rory disappeared.

She brushed her teeth and tossed a t-shirt on over her sports bra and walked back outside. Austin was already waxing the board.

"This is one of your personal sticks isn't it?" Austin grinned.

"Yeah. She's yours now, at least while you're here anyway. Make sure you coat her up good." Rory smiled, turning her head away from the woman kneeling in the sand. *I've never seen a rash guard and board shorts look so good.* She shook her head, concentrating on the line-up of waves instead of Austin's ass.

"Yes ma'am." Austin smiled as she watched Rory's eyes travel over her.

"All I want you to do is paddle out and watch the

line. You need to get used to the undertow, it's much stronger here. The bottom is a very sharp reef, so be careful. It's fairly deep, but you don't want to wipe out hard. The first thing we're going to work on is judgment and prediction."

"Okay." Austin watched the serious lines forming on Rory's face.

"I want you to judge each wave in every set. You need to be able to predict the composition of every wave before it even breaks on the line. That's all we're working on today. I want you to turn and paddle if you think it's a wave you would drop on, but don't stand, I want you to ride the wave in on your stomach. The second part of today's lesson is learning the strength and power of these waves. They're much stronger than anything you've ever been on. For now, all we're doing is learning the waves."

"I think I can handle it."

"Good. I expect you to do everything that I say and don't go ahead of me…"

"Rory, I trust you and I respect you tremendously. I won't stand up until you tell me."

"Alright. I'll be right back." Rory walked into the house and returned with a small digital video camera and a tripod.

"What's that for?"

"I'm going to set this up and record everything. Just do as I say. Judge the line and predict the best waves before they break. When I think you've had enough, we'll go inside and watch the tape. This is the best teaching tool I have ever seen."

"Sounds good." Austin took off into the water and Rory focused the camera in Austin's direction as she paddled out to the line.

~ ~ ~

Austin sat on the board, bobbing up and down like a cork in the water as the waves came and went. She studied the forming of the waves for close to twenty minutes, and then all of a sudden, she turned on the board and paddled into an oncoming wave as it lifted her and the board. She stayed on her stomach, riding the wave as her heart pounded wildly in her chest and adrenaline raced through her veins. She was overwhelmed by the speed and force of the water beneath her, nearly falling off before the wave finally flattened out. She paddled back out to wait and catch another one, over and over until Rory called her in. Austin rode her last wave as far as she could and paddled the rest of the way to the shore. She ran over to Rory with the board under her arm.

"Well, how did I do?"

"Not bad, want some lunch?"

"Hell yeah, I'm starving. Oh my God, Rory, those waves are unbelievable! I wasn't anticipating the power and just about fell off the first one."

Rory started making turkey sandwiches, while Austin pulled one of the barstools out from under the island in the kitchen. She put her dry towel over it and sat down.

"What do you do at home to keep in shape?" Rory asked.

"I go to the gym sometimes and run a lot around my neighborhood, but mostly my strength comes from working at the aquarium."

I want you to start running with me tomorrow. We'll

work out as we run. I used to go to one of the local gyms, but I'd prefer to stay away from the locals if that's alright with you."

"No, that's fine with me."

"Good," Rory said, handing her a sandwich. "We'll start with two miles and build up from there."

~ ~ ~

The next morning Austin met Rory in the sand for their Tai Chi routine. She was dressed very similarly to Rory, in a sports bra and workout shorts. *She's going to kill me dressed like that. As if the skin tight rash guard and tiny board shorts aren't enough, now she's practically naked!* Rory bit her bottom lip, shaking the thoughts from her head. Touching Austin in Australia had barely wet her appetite. The more time she spent around her, cooped up in the small house, the more she wanted her. She was afraid she may snap before their trip was over.

"Morning," Austin said, sliding into position next to her.

Rory nodded.

They went through their routine for the next hour, and then they put on their sneakers. Rory grabbed a small t-shirt to cover her upper body. Deciding that was probably a good idea, Austin put one on as well. Rory set the pace as they ran down the beach towards Waimea Bay. Rory knew that stretch of beach like the back of her hand and when she reached the half mile point, she stopped.

"We're going to drop down and do one set of twenty

five sit-ups, push-ups, burpees, and then jumping jacks," Rory said.

"Uh…okay." Austin dropped next to her in the sand.

They took turns counting reps to stay on pace until they'd finished. Both women had beads of sweat running down their faces and were covered in sand.

"Come on," Rory yelled as she took off running again.

They repeated the same routine until they'd ran two miles and completed one-hundred reps of each exercise. Austin's muscles were slightly sore as they arrived back at their starting point. She kicked her shoes off, tore away her socks and peeled her t-shirt off.

"I've never had this much sand in so many places," she grimaced.

Rory laughed and stepped around her, removing her own socks, shoes and t-shirt. She walked onto the side of the deck, pulling a thin metal chain. A shower of cool water washed over her, rinsing away the sand.

"Sweet!" Austin cheered, rushing over to her and squeezing under the spray.

Rory chuckled, stepping aside as Austin stretched under the water like a lazy cat in the sun.

"What's next almighty one?" Austin mocked Rory with a bow as they entered the house.

"Keep that up, smartass, and I'll have you swimming miles of shoreline like I used to do."

"You're kidding me?"

"No I'm not. You have to be in better than perfect shape, Austin. I was…and it wasn't…it wasn't good enough." Rory looked away, finishing in a whisper.

"Hey, I'll do whatever you say. I trust you," Austin said softly as she put her hand on Rory's cheek, turning her head until their eyes met. She wanted so badly to kiss the lips beckoning her. *Your gorgeous eyes take my breath away. You have no idea what you to do me, Rory.*

"How do you feel?" Rory asked, stepping away from Austin.

"Fine. Why?"

"Think you're ready to ride a wave or two?"

"Sure."

"Go get your board and change. I'll get the camera and meet you out there."

My board. My board that used to be her board. Could I possible ever give this stick a ride anywhere close to the ones she used to give it? Austin ran her hand over the wax on the light blue and green surfboard.

~ ~ ~

Rory had told Austin to take it easy, and stand up if and when she felt comfortable. Now, she held her breath, waiting for the woman in the water to paddle in and fearlessly drop on her first North Shore wave; the same woman that was slowly showing her how to live again.

Austin took a deep breath, paddling as hard as she could as the most beautiful break she'd ever seen picked the board up under her, rushing forward as she dropped on the face, popping up to her feet. She carved a little, but mostly just rode the face of the wave, reaching down and letting her left hand trail the water behind her. She was sure she'd held that deep breath until the ride was over. She felt an incredible sense of self pride. One of her lifelong dreams had just come true. Her heart pounded out of her chest and she fought back tears of joy as she paddled back out to do it all over again.

Rory's nerves were frazzled watching Austin ride wave after wave. She wiped the couple of tears that slid down her face. There was nothing like your first time and this was Austin first time riding a tube style, competition wave. This was the same beach and those were the same waves that she'd used to hone her own skills, learning how to become a champion.

After her fourth ride, Rory waved her arms and yelled for her to come back in. Austin came out of the water, jogging towards Rory. She tossed the board in the sand before jumping into Rory's arms. Rory had no time to react, much less brace herself, as she fell back into the sand with Austin on top of her. Their lips met as she wrapped her arms around Austin's waist, kissing her passionately. The weight of the slightly smaller woman on top of her was welcoming. The saltwater soaking her clothes was nothing compared to the flood between her legs. Rory felt the fire in her belly roar to life when she slid her hand under the thin material of the rash guard and over the silky smooth skin of Austin's back.

Austin moaned into the kiss, rocking her hips into Rory and sliding her wet thigh between her legs.

The sudden pressure on her center shocked Rory back to reality. She opened her eyes, rolling Austin off her in one fluid motion.

"What's wrong?" Austin panted.

"I can't. I'm sorry," Rory said as she stood up, walking away.

"Damn it. I know you want me. You've shown me how much you want me. You're fighting demons larger than I could ever imagine. If you would just open up and let me in...I can help you. Rory, we can fight them together," she said to the empty beach as she kicked her foot in the sand.

Chapter Fifteen

A week later, Austin was ripping waves every morning and afternoon. She continued to follow Rory's strict regime of Tai Chi. Then, they would do their running workout, adding more reps to each exercise, daily. Her body was becoming tighter and stronger than she'd ever seen it, and she was more focused mentally, than she could've ever imagined. Rory worked closely with her, teaching her every aspect that she could without actually getting into the water and riding the waves next to her.

They hadn't talked about their kiss in the sand. The one time Austin had tried to bring it up, Rory had changed the subject and gone to bed early. She was on the verge of giving up on ever getting Rory to open up to her. They still had one more week before the tournament and then they'd go back home and back to work, away from each other. She wondered if Rory would have anything to do with her once she joined the pro tour.

Austin sat on the deck, watching the sun slowly sink

into the ocean. Her dreams were coming true and her heart was breaking at the same time. She wiped the tears from her cheeks. The bittersweet feeling was sickening. She'd never felt more alone.

Rory walked outside with a beach blanket rolled up under her arm.

"Do you want to take a walk with me?" Rory asked, stopping next to Austin.

"Sure." Austin stood, following her lead through the dunes. Rory headed off in the opposite direction from the one they ran in each day. "We never go this way," Austin said, matching her slow pace.

"It's time," Rory replied, watching the sky as it began to darken.

Time for what? Austin shook her head. She wasn't in the mood for one of Rory's philosophical riddles.

They walked a mile down the beach in silence as the full moon rose high over in the night sky, illuminating the ocean. The hair on the back of Rory's neck stood up. Her skin was cold, despite the warm temperature of the evening. The roar of the waves crashing in the distance was deafening to her ears. Her chest constricted so tightly, she could barely breathe as she stopped walking and turned towards the water. She dropped the blanket in the sand, spreading it as she sat down.

Austin hadn't paid much attention to her surroundings. She'd been running on autopilot over the past few days, fighting her feelings for Rory and knowing their time together was coming to an end. She watched Rory sit down, tucking her knees against her chest as she wrapped her arms tightly around them. She raised an eyebrow at Rory's odd behavior and turned her head towards the water.

Austin stumbled, nearly falling on top of Rory as the largest wave she'd ever seen swelled in the distance, roaring loudly towards the shore, forming a perfect barrel. The face of the wave was close to ten feet tall and closing out quickly. She was stunned, literally speechless as she watched the next wave crest almost identically. She wasn't sure how long she'd been holding her breath from the shock of the incredible wave, but her heart raced with excitement.

"Oh my God," Austin finally muttered.

"Welcome to Bonzai Pipeline," Rory said softly. She pointed in the distance to the left. "Backdoor is right over there."

"Wow! This...it's incredible," Austin whispered.

"Underneath that majestic display of nature is a razor sharp reef with jagged rocks in very shallow water."

Austin turned her head, noticing the tears on Rory's cheeks, glistening in the moonlight. "Oh, Rory, I'm sorry," she said, wrapping her arms around the sobbing woman. She'd seen the video of Rory's accident and knew it had taken place right there on that very same wave.

Rory cried uncontrollably, mourning the loss of her spirit and her passion, and essentially, the loss of herself. Everything she had ever known had died in those waves crashing to shore in front of her. She hated them for swallowing her whole, taking everything from her and spitting out a shell of the person she used to be. It had taken her years of spiritual meditation to get over the anger and now, the hatred only made her feel empty with sadness. She ran her hand along the four inch scar on the left side of the top of her head, which had been a daily reminder of her tragic dance with the devil.

240

"We didn't need to come here," Austin murmured.

"Yes…yes I did," Rory wept. "I needed to do this." She allowed Austin to hold her as she wiped her eyes. "It's the only way I can move on," she sighed, as the last of the tears fell. "I have to let go."

She stared at the magnificent waves. They were just as beautiful as she'd remembered. "It's amazing how something so spectacular can literally rip your life right out from under you in less than a split second. A wave like that is unforgiving and it never looks back."

"I can't even begin to imagine what that was like," Austin whispered.

"I don't remember it," Rory sighed. "I actually don't remember the days leading up to the competition either. Martie and I were living in the beach house and traveling the world with the tour. We'd just returned from a pro event in Portugal. I was riding the high from that win and we were heading into Pipe Masters in a few weeks, which was the final event of the tour. I was leading the points up to that point and it was the first time that had happened in my career. I'd always done well at Pipe, winning all of my championships right here on these waves. Hell, how could I not? It was my own backyard." The corners of Rory's mouth tried to smile as she thought about the amazing times she'd had on that stretch of beach, winning multiple championships, but the smile never actually formed.

"We'd always surfed the Pipeline Invitational which was held two weeks before Pipe Masters every year. It was like easy practice and we looked forward to the event and finally coming home after traveling so much all year." She paused.

The last time I remember surfing wasn't even in this water. We had stopped in Brazil for a Boarder Classic at the last minute, which Martie won by the way, beating me by half a point. We joked about that all the way back to Hawaii. I teased her about letting her win one since I was pretty much about to wrap up my fourth title." Rory did smile then, thinking about the last time she and Martie had surfed together. "That's the last time I remember surfing."

"Wow," Austin replied. "That's...that sounds really special. At least your last memory is a good one."

"Yeah. So, I remember flying here and everything, but not really anything after that. Martie told me we surfed Pipe and Backdoor for the next three days straight. Then came the Invitational. I've seen all of the videos. I know the barrel had to be at least thirteen feet with the face of the wall topping out over fifteen. Pipe was going off that day. I think I read somewhere that those were record waves for the Invitational. Anyway, you've probably seen the video. I slid out in the mushy bottom and well, according to the reports, I hit my head on the reef and was held under the water for at least two minutes." Rory subconsciously rubbed the scar on her head.

"I died out there in that water," she sighed. "I have no idea why I'm sitting here, alive today. I owe my life to the extraordinary medics that brought me back to life in this very same spot."

Austin felt a chill run through her body.

"My body was revived, but I stopped living that day. When I awoke from the coma, I no longer felt the power of the ocean pulling me in and the call of the waves fell on deaf ears. It took me a while, but I learned to live this new life." Rory looked at Austin, who was sitting with her arm around Rory's waist.

"Then, I met you and my world turned upside down all over again."

Austin raised an eyebrow and Rory continued. "Life is like a game of poker. You're dealt one hand and given chips to play with. It's all about how well you bluff and play the game. I don't know why or how, but I truly believe I was dealt a new hand after going all in and losing everything in the last one. People generally don't get a second hand and I've been holding this hand very close, barely playing any of my chips. You entered the game and began calling my bluff over and over, tempting me to go all in. Bloody hell, you scare me to death."

Rory ran her hand over Austin's cheek.

"You came into my life for a reason, Austin. You…" Rory paused. "I hear the waves and feel the ocean for the first time in years. I can't explain it, but somehow you made me feel alive again. You've awakened the soul inside me that I thought was dead and gone. You excite me, terrify me, and drive me wild all at the same time. I've fought this for so long and I'm done. You win," she whispered, leaning forward and pressing her lips to Austin's.

The kiss was gentle and probing at first, but heated quickly as Rory pushed Austin onto her back, sliding her hand under her t-shirt and over the silky smooth skin of her taut stomach from the waistband of her shorts to the bottom curve of her breasts. The moonlight cast a soft glow around them and the massive waves in the distance crashed against the shore, drowning out the soft moans echoing between them.

Austin rolled Rory onto her back, pushing her shirt up as she ran her tongue over the soft skin around her belly button. Rory hissed, watching the gray eyes looking at her, as Austin moved up her body, laying half on top of her. Rory reached down, running her hand down Austin's waist to her hip, then over her tight ass. Austin gasped, feeling herself growing wetter as she moved against the woman under her.

Rory slipped her hand under the bottom of Austin's shorts, sliding it up her thigh as Austin pushed her hand under the waistband of Rory's shorts. Each woman found what she was searching for. Austin kissed Rory passionately as she slid her fingers inside of Rory for the first time. Rory pulled away from the kiss, groaning with pleasure. Austin felt so good inside of her. Rory slipped her fingers through Austin's wet folds, easing inside, matching her stroke for stroke.

Their lips met frantically once again, tongues danced and teeth nibbled, fanning the flames of the fire burning between them. They thrust into each other roughly, grinding faster and harder until they were panting, gasping for breath and climbing the walls of desire.

Rory came first, crying out into the night as her body convulsed. Austin groaned loudly, collapsing on top of her. Their hearts pounded together as they floated slowly back to reality.

Rory rolled Austin to the side, sitting up slightly. "Did I hurt you?" she asked.

"Really?" Austin shook her head, running her hand through her hair to push it out of her face. "If you don't stop asking me that, I'm going to hurt *you.*"

Rory smiled.

"You have no idea what you do to me. I…I've never

loved anything as much as surfing and I thought that love had died. I found it again when you came into my life. Austin, I found it in *you*. I love you so much that it hurts to breathe," she whispered.

"I love you too," Austin said, closing the space between them and kissing her with a little more intensity than she'd meant to. Rory returned the kiss, pushing Austin onto her back before pulling away slightly.

Staring down into deep gray eyes, she said, "We better get out of here before we get caught. There are houses on the other side of those dunes."

Austin grinned, biting her lower lip between her teeth seductively.

"I knew you were trouble the moment I laid eyes on you," Rory laughed, getting up and pulling Austin to her feet. They stood on wobbly legs for a second as the blood rushed back down.

"Is that so?" Austin teased.

"Yes. Now, come on." Rory folded up the blanket and walked down to the water. She stepped in, allowing the warm water to cascade around her calves as she reached around her neck, removing the pendant.

Austin watched from a few feet away as Rory stretched her back, tossing something way out into the surf.

"What was that?" Austin asked.

"Letting go," Rory smiled.

Austin shrugged and fell instep next to her as they walked back up the beach towards the house.

~ ~ ~

Three days later, Rory watched from the shore as the final round began. Each of the four surfers in the water was wearing a different color rash guard. Austin was out in the line-up, sitting on her board in a hot pink one. She'd barely made it out of the first heat, catching only two waves and wiping out hard on the first one. Her second heat had been much better and she scored high enough to make the final round.

You can do this. Concentrate, Austin. Find your center. Go...go damn it! She saw the perfect swell coming towards her and began paddling as hard as she could, dropping on the face of the wave. She carved quickly to her right, riding up the face of the wave into a snap, then a floater along the lip of the wave before tail sliding back inside. She carved up and down the face of the wave laying back on the board to drag her hand through the water before dumping off as the wave flattened out. She did a quick duck dive under another wave and paddled back out to the line.

Two more surfers rode the next pair of waves and the forth surfer saw Austin prepare to paddle for the swell behind them and she took off paddling to cut in on her. Austin saw her and backed off the wave. The girl rode half of the wave before wiping out. Rory had seen the entire incident and cheered loudly when she saw Austin make the right choice. If she'd popped up, the other girl would've run right over her.

The horn sounded a short blast, signaling one more minute in the heat. Austin watched the line-up closely, waiting as each wave rippled past her, until she saw the one she wanted. She paddled hard and dropped on the wave. Once again, performing a few smaller maneuvers along the face of the wave, then she cut back, using her speed to pop her up off the lip of the wave into an aerial. She held her hand on the edge of the board as it slid sideways in the air, then back down on the rail, slicing through the water. She rode back up the wave into a floating tail slide, before dumping off the back of the wave when the long blast of the horn indicated the heat had ended.

The scores were being tallied as the surfers paddled in. Rory stood near the judge's booth, waiting patiently. She'd been wearing a ball cap and dark sunglasses the entire day, trying desperately to not get recognized.

"This is a huge surprise. Rory Eden has returned to the North Shore," the young guy next to her held up his camera. "This is going to be the comeback story of the decade."

"I'm not..." Rory was cut off by the loudspeaker as the results were announced. Austin had just set her board down in the sand as her name was called out in first place. The official standing nearby slipped the medal over her head and she took off, jogging towards Rory, screaming with excitement.

"That's who you should be interviewing," Rory said. "She's going to be better than I ever was."

The reporter flashed the camera the second that Austin flung herself into Rory's arms, kissing her deeply.

"I love you so damn much, Rory Eden!" Austin grinned.

"Care to comment now?" he asked.

Rory laughed. "I think you just outed me," she said to Austin, smiling and kissing her again.

About the Author

Graysen Morgen is the bestselling author of *Falling Snow*, *Fast Pitch*, and *Bridesmaid of Honor*, as well as many other titles. She was born and raised in North Florida with winding rivers and waterways at her back door and the white sandy beach a mile away. She has spent most of her lifetime in the sun and on the water. She enjoys reading, writing, fishing, and spending as much time as possible with her partner and their daughter.

You can contact Graysen at graysenmorgen@aol.com and like her fan page on facebook.com/graysenmorgen.

Go to www.tri-pub.com to get information about Triplicity Publishing or to submit your manuscript.

Other Titles Available From Triplicity Publishing

Bridesmaid of Honor by Graysen Morgen. Britton Prescott's best friend is getting married and she's the maid of honor. As if that isn't enough to deal with, Britton's sister announces she's getting married in the same month and her maid of honor is her best friend Daphne, the same woman who has tormented Britton for years. Britton has to suck it up and play nice, instead of scratching her eyes out, because she and Daphne are in both weddings. Everyone is counting on them to behave like adults.

Falling Snow by Graysen Morgen. Dr. Cason Macauley, a high-speed trauma surgeon from Denver meets Adler Troy, a professional snowboarder and sparks fly. The last thing Cason wants is a relationship and Adler doesn't realize what's right in front of her until it's gone, but will it be too late?

Fate vs. Destiny by Graysen Morgen. Logan Greer devotes her life to investigating plane crashes for the National Transportation Safety Board. Brooke McCabe is an investigator with the Federal Aviation Association who literally flies by the seat of her pants. When Logan gets tangled in head games with both women will she choose fate or destiny?

Just Me by Graysen Morgen. Wild child Ian Wiley has to grow up and take the reins of the hundred year old family business when tragedy strikes. Cassidy Harland is a little surprised that she came within an inch of picking up a gorgeous stranger in a bar and is shocked to find out that stranger is the new head of her company.

Love Loss Revenge by Graysen Morgen. Rian Casey is an FBI Agent working the biggest case of her career and madly in love with her girlfriend. Her world is turned upside when tragedy strikes. Heartbroken, she tries to rebuild her life. When she discovers the truth behind what really happened that awful night she decides justice isn't good enough, and vows revenge on everyone involved.

Natural Instinct by Graysen Morgen. Chandler Scott is a Marine Biologist who keeps her private life private. Corey Joslen is intrigued by Chandler from the moment she meets her. Chandler is forced to finally open her life up to Corey. It backfires in Corey's face and sends her running. Will either woman learn to trust her natural instinct?

Secluded Heart by Graysen Morgen. Chase Leery is an overworked cardiac surgeon with a group of best friends that have an opinion and a reason for everything. When she meets a new artist named Remy Sheridan at her best friend's art gallery she is captivated by the reclusive woman. When Chase finds out why Remy is so sheltered will she put her career on the line to help her or is it too difficult to love someone with a secluded heart?

In Love, at War by Graysen Morgen. Charley Hayes is in the Army Air Force and stationed at Ford Island in Pearl Harbor. She is the commanding officer of her own female-only service squadron and doing the one thing she loves most, repairing airplanes. Life is good for Charley, until the day she finds herself falling in love while fighting for her life as her country is thrown haphazardly into World War II. Can she survive being in love and at war?

Fast Pitch by Graysen Morgen. Graham Cahill is a senior in college and the catcher and captain of the softball team. Despite being an all-star pitcher, Bailey Michaels is young and arrogant. Graham and Bailey are forced to get to know each other off the field in order to learn to work together on the field. Will the extra time pay off or will it drive a nail through the team?

Submerged by Graysen Morgen. Assistant District Attorney Layne Carmichael had no idea that the sexy woman she took home from a local bar for a one night stand would turn out to be someone she would be prosecuting months later. Scooter is a Naval Officer on a submarine who changes women like she changes uniforms. When she is accused of a heinous crime she is shocked to see her latest conquest sitting across from her as the prosecuting attorney.

Vow of Solitude by Austen Thorne. Detective Jordan Denali is in a fight for her life against the ghosts from her past and a Serial Killer taunting her with his every move. She lives a life of solitude and plans to keep it that way. When Callie Marceau, a curious Medical Examiner, decides she wants in on the biggest case of her career, as well as, Jordan's life, Jordan is powerless to stop her.

Igniting Temptation by Sydney Canyon. Mackenzie Trotter is the Head of Pediatrics at the local hospital. Her life takes a rather unexpected turn when she meets a flirtatious, beautiful fire fighter. Both women soon discover it doesn't take much to ignite temptation.

One Night by Sydney Canyon. While on a business trip, Caylen Jarrett spends an amazing night with a beautiful stripper. Months later, she is shocked and confused when that same woman re-enters her life. The fact that this stranger could destroy her career doesn't bother her. C.J. is more terrified of the feelings this woman stirs in her. Could she have fallen in love in one night and not even known it?

Fine by Sydney Canyon. Collin Anderson hides behind a façade, pretending everything is fine. Her workaholic wife and best friend are both oblivious as she goes on an emotional journey, battling a potentially hereditary disease that her mother has been diagnosed with. The only person who knows what is really going on, is Collin's doctor. The same doctor, who is an acquaintance that she's always been attracted to, and who has a partner of her own.

Shadow's Eyes by Sydney Canyon. Tyler McCain is the owner of a large ranch that breeds and sells different types of horses. She isn't exactly thrilled when a Hollywood movie producer shows up wanting to film his latest movie on her property.
Reegan Delsol is an up and coming actress who has everything going for her when she lands the lead role in a

new film, but there one small problem that could blow the entire picture.